FIFTH-GRADE ZOMBIES

GOOSEBUMPS®
HALL OF HORRORS

#1 CLAWS!
#2 NIGHT OF THE GIANT EVERYTHING
#3 SPECIAL EDITION: THE FIVE MASKS OF DR. SCREEM
#4 WHY I QUIT ZOMBIE SCHOOL
#5 DON'T SCREAM!
#6 THE BIRTHDAY PARTY OF NO RETURN

GOOSEBUMPS®
MOST WANTED

#1 PLANET OF THE LAWN GNOMES
#2 SON OF SLAPPY
#3 HOW I MET MY MONSTER
#4 FRANKENSTEIN'S DOG
#5 DR. MANIAC WILL SEE YOU NOW
#6 CREATURE TEACHER: FINAL EXAM
#7 A NIGHTMARE ON CLOWN STREET
#8 NIGHT OF THE PUPPET PEOPLE
#9 HERE COMES THE SHAGGEDY
#10 THE LIZARD OF OZ

SPECIAL EDITION #1 ZOMBIE HALLOWEEN
SPECIAL EDITION #2 THE 12 SCREAMS OF CHRISTMAS
SPECIAL EDITION #3 TRICK OR TRAP
SPECIAL EDITION #4 THE HAUNTER

GOOSEBUMPS®
SLAPPYWORLD

#1 SLAPPY BIRTHDAY TO YOU
#2 ATTACK OF THE JACK!
#3 I AM SLAPPY'S EVIL TWIN
#4 PLEASE DO NOT FEED THE WEIRDO
#5 ESCAPE FROM SHUDDER MANSION
#6 THE GHOST OF SLAPPY
#7 IT'S ALIVE! IT'S ALIVE!
#8 THE DUMMY MEETS THE MUMMY!
#9 REVENGE OF THE INVISIBLE BOY
#10 DIARY OF A DUMMY
#11 THEY CALL ME THE NIGHT HOWLER!
#12 MY FRIEND SLAPPY
#13 MONSTER BLOOD IS BACK

FIFTH-GRADE ZOMBIES

R.L. STINE

SCHOLASTIC INC.

Goosebumps book series created by Parachute Press, Inc.
Copyright © 2021 by Scholastic Inc.

ISBN 978-1-338-35581-9

10 9 8 7 6 5 4 3 2 1   21 22 23 24 25

Printed in the U.S.A.   40
First printing 2021

SLAPPY HERE, EVERYONE

Welcome to My World.

Yes, it's *SlappyWorld*—you're only *screaming* in it! Hahaha.

Here's a question for you: Do you know why people call me Slappy?

Because that's my NAME! Haha.

That's an easy question that you flunked. It brings me to a second question: Who is smarter—you or a dummy? Ha. I can't believe I'm smarter than you—and I have a *wooden head*!

So, don't call me Dummy, Dummy. I'm so smart, I can read the words in my alphabet soup! Haha.

Do me a favor. Turn sideways.

I *knew* it. I can look through your ears and see sunlight on the other side!

Did you ever think of buying a brain? I hear *thinking* can be a lot of fun.

But don't worry. You've got a good head on your shoulders. It keeps your cap from falling off!

1

Haha. Do you know why I like to tease you so much?

Because you *deserve* it! Hahaha.

Now, here's a story about a boy named Todd Coates.

Todd is a city kid from New York, and he is on his way to stay with his cousins on a farm in Wisconsin. Todd thinks he may get bored.

Wow, is *he* wrong!

You'll never guess what he's going to find when the full moon rises over the cornfield. Here's a hint: I call this story *Fifth-Grade Zombies*.

I'll let my friend Todd tell you all about it.

It's just one more terrifying tale from *SlappyWorld*.

1

Well, do you believe it?

Here I am, Todd Coates, a city kid my whole life, from Queens, New York. I'm bouncing on a bus through Wisconsin Dells, on a narrow, bumpy country road. Watching the trees blur past. And the fields . . . the dry brown farm fields stretching toward who-knows-where.

Todd Coates. From the Greatest City on Earth. The Big Apple. On my way to living on a farm for a year. Is that possible?

The only farms I've ever seen were in the movies. They looked like living on Mars to me. I mean, where do the farm people go for good Thai food? And do they have Wi-Fi?

I'm not a nature guy. Maybe you've guessed that. Sure, I see trees when I'm Rollerblading in the park. But I'm not sure I've ever even touched a tree.

I lie in my bed at night and listen to the garbage trucks out on the street. The whine and growl of garbage trucks are like a lullaby to a city kid like me. But farm life? I couldn't picture it.

Guess what? I had nightmares about the farm. I saw myself sleeping on a pile of hay with chickens pecking at my pajamas.

But don't get me started about nightmares.

Anyway, here I was, on this squeaky bus, on this county road, sunlight and shadows rolling across the windows. We passed the town of Baraboo, so I knew we were getting close. My cousins' farm is about twenty miles west of Baraboo. It's near a town called Moose Hollow, so small it's not even on the map. Believe that?

I don't mean to make fun. My aunt Clara and uncle Jake are great people. When my parents had to go off on their long business trip, they were the only ones in my family who could take me.

Aunt Clara said it would be an educational year for me.

She got that right!

I didn't know my cousins Mila and Skipper very well. But I was glad I wouldn't be the only kid on the farm. Mila is my age, twelve. And Skipper is a few years older.

I FaceTimed with them a few times. Mila seemed nice. A little quiet and shy. Aunt Clara likes to gush. I mean, she's always rah-rah like a cheerleader. I think she could get excited over Corn Flakes in the morning.

Uncle Jake was the opposite. He kept scratching

his cheeks and clearing his throat and muttering away from the phone. I guess he doesn't like FaceTime.

And Skipper was weird, too. He's about a foot taller than everyone else in the family. He has a croaky voice, like it's still changing. And he seemed really tense. He kept blinking a lot and glancing around. I don't know what his problem was.

The second time I FaceTimed with Skipper, he slid his face up real close to the screen, and he whispered, "Todd, don't believe everything you hear."

How weird was that?

I mean, I hadn't heard *anything at all*.

Do you think he was trying to scare me?

The bus hit a hard bump, and I nearly went flying from my seat. It was late afternoon, and the shadows across the farm fields were stretching longer.

I pulled my phone from my jeans pocket and tried to call Mom and Dad back in New York. They were still home. They weren't leaving on their trip till the weekend.

But all I got was silence. No cell service way out here in the wilderness. I couldn't even send a text.

I slid the phone back into my pocket and pulled out my harmonica. My stomach was starting to feel fluttery. I could feel myself growing tense as we came closer to Moose Hollow. And one thing that always helped to calm me down was to blow a little blues on my harp.

It's not anything fancy. It's a Hohner Special 20 in the key of C. Sort of a beginner's harmonica.

My parents bought it for me for my eleventh birthday.

I've spent so many hours practicing on it that I should be a lot better. But I don't care. Playing the instrument always makes me feel good.

I brought two special things with me to the farm. One was the harmonica. The other was a red plastic lighter. I never light the thing. I don't even know if it will flame anymore. My grandpa Dave gave it to me a few days before he died. He carried it with him everywhere. Always in his pocket. Maybe he even slept with it. I don't know. I do know he thought it was special. So I've treasured it as a good-luck charm ever since.

I gripped my harmonica and squinted out the dusty bus window at the passing fields. What were those animals poking up from the dirt? They weren't squirrels, and they weren't rabbits.

Maybe I really *had* traveled to another planet!

I raised the harmonica to my mouth, slid it back and forth a few times—and started to play. I don't really play songs on it. I sort of free-form it. I like to get a rhythm going and then impro- vise a melody.

I was pumping out some pretty good sounds when a shout made me stop. It was the bus driver up at the front. He was a red-faced old guy with a blue-and-white bandanna tied around his bald head.

"Put that away, kid," he called. "In your pocket, okay?"

"I was playing softly," I said. I sat halfway to the back, so I had to shout.

"Don't give me any mouth, okay?" he growled. "You're annoying the other passengers."

I glanced around the bus. "There's only one other passenger," I said. "And he's asleep."

"Okay, I heard that," the driver said. He pulled the bus to the side of the road. The brakes squeaked to a stop. He climbed up from his seat and stepped into the aisle. He motioned to me. "Out," he said. "You're out."

He pushed a button and the bus door slid open.

"Huh?" I said. "Excuse me?"

"You're out," he repeated, pointing to the open door. "Come on. Let's go."

My heart started to pound. I jumped to my feet. I gripped the harmonica tightly in my hand. "Huh? I don't understand—" I started.

He climbed down the bus steps. "I'll get your suitcase."

"But—but—" I sputtered.

"It's your stop," he said. "Moose Hollow." He pointed to a red truck parked by the trees. "I see some people waiting for you."

"Oh!" I saw the truck doors open. Uncle Jake and Aunt Clara hurried out, waving to me. Mila and Skipper were in the truck bed. They leaped down to the ground and came running toward the bus.

Everyone hugged everyone.

The driver slid open the compartment on the side of the bus and pulled out my suitcase. He shoved it into Uncle Jake's hands.

"He isn't much of a musician," the driver told my uncle. He adjusted the bandanna around his bald head. "Just sayin'."

He climbed back onto the bus and shut the door.

Uncle Jake ran his fingers through his hair. "What did he mean by that?"

I shrugged. "Beats me."

The bus started with a hard jolt, then rumbled away.

Aunt Clara brushed back a strand of her coppery hair. "Todd, I can't believe you're here," she said.

I gazed around at the trees and the flat brown field that stretched across the road. "I can't, either," I said. "It's like a million miles from New York."

"Two million," Skipper said. He kicked a clump of dirt in front of his brown leather boot. "Todd, you ever see that old TV show *The Twilight Zone*?" He didn't wait for me to answer. "Well, you're *in* it!"

My aunt and uncle laughed. But Mila just shook her head. She elbowed her brother in the ribs. "Shut up, Skipper. Give us a break."

Skipper giggled. He had a high, scratchy laugh. Like a bird or something. It didn't sound right coming from such a big, tall guy.

He kept shifting his weight from one long leg to the other. As if it was hard for him to stand still.

Aunt Clara shivered. She tightened her red-and-black flannel jacket around her. "Feel the chill in the air? You can tell it isn't summer anymore."

"Farm people like to talk about the weather a lot," Uncle Jake said.

"We don't have weather in New York," I said. It was a joke. I thought it was pretty funny. But they all just stared at me.

Skipper turned and started to take long strides to the truck. "We'd better hurry home," he said. "It's time to milk the horses."

He stared at me, waiting for me to react. I guess he wanted to see if I believed him or not.

Mila stepped up beside me. "My brother has a twisted sense of humor," she said in a low voice.

"At least I *have* a sense of humor," Skipper snapped. He wrapped both hands around the side of the truck bed and hoisted himself inside. "Mila is the sensitive type," he continued. "She thinks it hurts an ear of corn when you boil it!"

He laughed at his own joke.

Mila scowled and made a *grrrr* sound.

Skipper reached both hands down to help me into the truck. But I grabbed the side and pulled myself up beside him.

Mila climbed in from the other side. A strong gust of wind caught her light brown hair and sent it flying behind her head like a flag. She pulled a Chicago Cubs cap from her pocket and slid it down over her hair.

"Hold on to the side, Todd," Uncle Jake called from behind the wheel. "Have you ever ridden in a truck before?"

11

"Not really," I replied. "When I was little, Mom and Dad took me to the New York auto show, and I would climb into all the trucks."

Skipper grinned. "That doesn't count."

"Most people don't have cars out here," Mila said. "Just SUVs and trucks. Cars aren't very good when the snow comes."

The truck started up with a roar, and we bounced onto the narrow county road. I gripped the side of the truck and tightened my leg muscles as we picked up speed.

"Are you okay?" Skipper shouted over the powerful wind. "You're not frightened, are you?"

"Hey, I ride the subways back home," I told him. "This isn't bad at all!"

The afternoon sun had fallen below the horizon. The fields stretched gray and purple in the evening light.

Mila had her phone out and was squinting at it as she typed with both thumbs. She raised her eyes. "It's my friend Shameka," she told me. "She just wants to know if you arrived."

"Shameka has a crush on you," Skipper said, grinning again.

"She hasn't met me," I said.

His grin grew wider. "So?"

I nearly lost my balance as Uncle Jake brought the truck around a curve. Out in the dark field, I saw those animals again. Their heads poked up between the dirt rows.

I squinted into the dim light. They weren't squirrels. And they weren't chipmunks.

"What are those?" I asked Skipper. I pointed. "See them? The little heads poking up?"

He followed my gaze. "They're field rats," he answered.

"Field rats? But—they're so big!"

He nodded. "Yeah. You've got to watch out for them, Todd. They're all diseased."

I blinked. "Diseased?"

"Seriously. They're all rabid," he said. "They have a kind of venom."

His eyes locked on mine. "Let's say you're out in a field, and one of them bites you. If that happens, you have less than thirty minutes to get an antidote. Or else your body just freezes up and you *die*."

I gasped. "Well, where do you keep the antidote?" I demanded.

"We don't have any," he said.

4

Across the truck bed from me, Mila rolled her eyes. "Skipper—" she started.

But we bounced hard as Uncle Jake turned the truck off the county road, onto a gravel path. She didn't finish what she had started to say.

I held on to the side and studied Skipper. He had to be kidding about the field rats—right?

I had news for him. We city kids don't scare easily.

"We're home," Mila said. She pointed to two tall silos. "That one is the grain silo, Todd. The other one is crop storage."

I nodded. *Crop storage?* What was she talking about?

We passed a dark-shingled barn, standing black against the darkening sky. "The stable is on the other side of the barn," Mila explained. "Have you ever ridden a horse?"

I smiled. "I rode a pony at my fifth birthday party," I said.

She and Skipper both laughed.

I eased my grip on the truck as we slowed down. My legs felt rubbery and my muscles ached. I couldn't wait to stand on solid ground.

"That's the chicken coop over there," Skipper said. "Do you hear them clucking their little heads off? That's where you'll be sleeping."

"Haha. Funny." Mila rolled her eyes again. "I know you're going to lighten up on Todd soon—aren't you?"

Skipper reached out a fist and bumped knuckles with me. "We're going to be best buds," he said.

Was he being sarcastic? I couldn't tell.

"We only have a few dozen chickens," Mila said. "Wait till you see Shameka's chicken coop. It's totally modern. Like from a sci-fi movie or something."

"The chickens are all robots," Skipper joked.

The truck bumped to a stop. The three of us jumped out. I bent my legs and stretched my arms above my head.

Aunt Clara stepped up beside me, fiddling with the sleeves of her flannel jacket. "Long day, Todd?"

I nodded. "The bus ride seemed endless."

Uncle Jake lifted my suitcase from the truck bed. "We'll get you up to your room to unpack. Then we'll have some dinner. You must be starving."

My shoes slid on the gravel driveway as I followed them to the house. "What do you eat here in Wisconsin? Is it true you eat only cheese and bratwurst?"

They laughed. "You've been doing your research!" my aunt said.

"Well, you can't order out like in New York City," Uncle Jake said. "But we have all kinds of good, fresh food."

"The corn was amazing this summer," Aunt Clara said. She pointed. "The cornfield starts back there. We had fresh sweet corn every night."

"There are pretty good restaurants in Baraboo," Skipper said. "It's only a half-hour drive."

"Wisconsin pizza is the best!" Mila exclaimed.

"Because the cheese is so good?" I said.

They laughed again. I was starting to feel a little more comfortable.

I stopped and gazed at the house. It wasn't what I had imagined. I guess I pictured a little old farmhouse, like in the movies. With bales of hay piled up in front and a rain barrel to collect water.

But this house was more like a mansion. Spread out behind neatly trimmed bushes. It was gray-shingled like the barn, wide and tall, with freshly painted shutters on the many windows. I saw a dim, rosy-colored light in a high window cut into the sloping roof. Two chimneys poked up on either end of the house.

A screened-in porch stood at one side of the front door. I saw a wicker porch swing and several big chairs. The door was painted bright yellow. Lights blazed in the wide front windows, sending an orange glow onto the front lawn.

Uncle Jake handed my suitcase to Skipper. "Take Todd up to his room," he said. "Your mom and I will get dinner on the table."

"Do I have to go up to the attic?" Skipper said. "It's creepy up there."

Mila gave him a shove toward the stairs. "You think you're funny, but you're just a loser."

Skipper nodded. "Okay, okay. No more jokes," he said. He raised his right hand. "I swear."

He started up the steep wooden staircase, and I followed him. The house was warm and smelled of freshly baked bread.

The air grew even warmer as we reached the second-floor landing. I followed him down a long hallway to the attic stairs at the other end.

"These are bedrooms and my mom's study," he explained. "Mom is taking online courses at the ag school. So she spends a lot of time in her study reading about plants, animals, and farming."

He glanced back at me. "Mom has the best Wi-Fi. So sometimes I sneak into her study and play *Minecraft* on her computer. Don't tell."

The narrow wooden steps leading up to the attic creaked and cracked under our shoes. "It's just one room up here," Skipper explained.

"Awesome," I said. "My own private hiding place."

"I used to come up here when I was a kid,"

Skipper said. "I'd look down from the window and pretend I was at the top of a tall mast on a pirate ship."

A dim, rose-colored light washed over us as we stepped into the room. I realized I was gazing at the attic window I had seen from the ground.

The room was small, just big enough for a narrow twin bed, a nightstand, a dresser, and a small desk. The low ceiling came to a point since we were just under the slanting roof.

I squinted, waiting for my eyes to adjust to the dim light.

And then I gasped.

A lump under the bed quilt. An arm tumbling out.

"Skipper—!" I grabbed his shoulder. "S-someone's in the bed!" I stammered.

His eyes went wide. He let my suitcase fall to the floor. "Oh no," he whispered. "This is where he was. We couldn't find him. We couldn't find him for months. He must be . . . he must be . . . *dead*."

5

We both froze for a moment. The strange pink light shimmered in my eyes. The bump under the bed quilt went in and out of focus.

And then Skipper dove forward. With two long strides, he grabbed the bed quilt in both hands— and tore it away. He bent quickly, raised the body high—and *heaved* it at me!

I caught it and staggered back to the doorway.

And then his laughter rang off the walls of the tiny attic room.

My heart thudding in my chest, I gazed at the scarecrow in my arms.

I stared at the straw arms poking out from the sleeves of an old raincoat. And the head ... a stained pillowcase with two big round black eyes gazing up at me.

A scarecrow.

Skipper was still laughing when Mila pushed her way into the room. She saw the straw figure in my arms. Saw the horrified look on my face. Saw her laughing brother.

"Skipper, you didn't," she muttered.

Skipper laughed some more. "Yes, I did."

Mila ripped the scarecrow from my arms and tossed it at him with all her strength. He caught it and fell back onto the bed, giggling that shrill giggle of his.

Mila shook her head. "Sorry, Todd," she said. "You weren't really scared—were you?"

"Of course not," I lied. "I'm getting used to Skipper's jokes."

Skipper tossed the scarecrow at Mila. She let it fall to the floor.

"Does he do this to everyone?" I asked. "Or just me?"

"Everyone," she answered. She scowled at Skipper. "You're giving Todd a great welcome. Why don't you act your age?"

"Why don't *you*?" he snapped back.

Mila kicked the scarecrow. It bounced a few feet across the floor. She turned to me. "I've lived on a farm my whole life," she said, "and I still think scarecrows are gross and creepy."

"*You're* gross and creepy," Skipper told her.

He picked up the scarecrow and held it so it appeared to stand on two feet. "Todd," he said, "once a scarecrow came to life in the cornfield. It started staggering toward our house. I'm serious."

He moved the scarecrow a few steps closer to me.

"We had to burn it before anyone saw it," he said. "We set it on fire. You should have heard its screams."

A hush fell over the room.

I stared hard at Skipper.

What is his problem?

Two nights later, my aunt and uncle made roast chicken and mashed potatoes for dinner. "We never give our chickens names," Uncle Jake said, "because we know we're probably going to eat them."

The food was great. I was starting to feel like part of the family. Skipper hadn't teased me or played any mean jokes on me since yesterday. And Mila was excited to show me every part of the farm.

After dinner, I climbed up to my attic room. I stretched out on my bed, pulled out my harmonica, and started to play some blues. Bursts of wind made my window rattle, a nice rhythm to my music.

I was feeling good. Sure, I missed Mom and Dad. But there was something awesome about beginning a whole new life in a totally different place.

I was pumping away on the harp. Really into it, my eyes shut, my breath coming fast and hard. Feeling it.

"What is that shrill noise?" a voice asked.

I nearly dropped the harmonica. I opened my eyes to see Mila standing in the doorway.

"It isn't noise," I said. "It's my harmonica." I held it up so she could see it.

"I thought you were choking on something," she said, stepping into the room.

"Haha," I said. "Funny. What kind of music do *you* like?"

"Oh. That was *music*?" she replied. "Sorry. I couldn't tell."

"It's called the blues," I said.

She rubbed her ears. "It was so loud, I couldn't tell *what* it was. Look. I think my ears are bleeding."

I set the harmonica down on my nightstand. "Remind me to play baby lullabies next time," I muttered.

Mila grabbed my hand and tried to tug me off the bed. "Come with me."

I pulled back. "Where are we going?"

"Someplace special. You have to see it."

"Where?" I demanded. "I already saw the threshing machine. I still haven't gotten over the excitement."

She slapped my arm. "Shut up, Todd. I'm taking you into the cornfield."

I squinted at her. "Why?"

"Because it's the harvest moon tonight," she answered. "Have you ever seen the harvest moon from a cornfield at night?"

"Back home, I did it every Tuesday," I said.

She made that *grrrrr* sound again. She did it a lot. "Trust me. You've never seen anything like it. It's like . . . magic."

I sighed and slid off the bed. I pulled a sweatshirt over my shirt. "Do you always get your way?" I asked.

"Only when I'm right," she replied.

I followed her down the stairs and out the front door. The sky was inky black. The cornfield appeared like a shimmering dark wall ahead of us.

I shivered. "It's cold," I murmured.

"That's part of the fun," Mila said.

Our shoes crunched over the ground. The dew had frozen into a layer of thin ice. A thread of orange light spread over the top of the field.

"That's the moonlight," Mila whispered. "Wait till it rises over the cornfield. It's so awesome."

We stepped up to the tall stalks, nearly two feet above my head. They cracked and crackled and buzzed as they swayed from side to side in the cold breeze.

I stopped. "Are there snakes in here?" My voice came out muffled in the cold air.

"Probably," Mila said. "But they won't hurt you. Just don't step on them."

I felt a cold tingle at the back of my neck. *Why do I suddenly feel very afraid?*

7

The wind shifted, and the stalks suddenly leaned toward us, as if reaching out to us. *They're alive!* I thought. *They're coming to grab me!*

The rattling along the ground sounded like a thousand rattlesnakes.

"Don't look so scared," Mila said. "This is supposed to be fun."

"But—" I started.

"The stalks rattle because they're dry and empty," she explained. "The corn has all been harvested. The stalks are like . . . skeletons."

I hugged the sleeves of my sweatshirt. "Are you trying to scare me?" I asked.

She shook her head. "No way. Wait till you see how cool this is."

"You didn't have to mention skeletons," I said. "You're starting to sound like Skipper."

"I don't know what Skipper's problem is," Mila said. "He was really looking forward to you coming here."

"Yeah. So he could scare me to death," I said.

She frowned. "Just follow me."

We ducked our heads and slid between the tall, swaying stalks. Our shoes scraped over a blanket of dead husks. Inside the tight rows of cornstalks, it suddenly felt warmer.

"Doesn't it smell awesome?" Mila said, a few feet ahead of me. "So fresh!"

"Awesome," I said. I lowered my shoulder to push stalks out of my way.

I gazed up, over the empty corn husks. Deep orange moonlight washed over the field, brightening the sky.

Mila motioned me forward. "This way," she said. "There's a small opening, and you can see the moon come up."

I slapped a bug off my neck. My shoes slipped on the husks on the ground, and I stumbled forward. I grabbed a stalk with both hands to keep from falling.

"Hurry," Mila whispered.

I stepped up beside her. We stood in a small opening, a break in the field. And I followed her gaze to the patch of sky ahead of us.

"Oh, wow," I muttered. And stared at an enormous orange moon, round at the top and cut off by the horizon. Floating slowly up into the reddening sky, rising like a huge hot-air balloon.

"It looks so close," I said. "Like it's touching the ground."

Mila smiled in reply. "You can't see this back in New York," she said. The orange moonlight reflected in her eyes and made her hair appear to shimmer like gold.

"Wow," I said again. "You were right. It's amazing."

The moon floated higher, and now it was a perfect orange ball, glowing over the endless cornfield.

"Let's keep walking," Mila said. She grabbed my arm and tugged me back into the tall stalks. "You have to see the tricks the moonlight plays in the field."

I stumbled again but caught my balance. I had to hurry to keep up with her. Despite the cold air, I mopped warm sweat off my forehead.

Narrow rivers of red-orange light washed along the ground. The cornstalks rose over me. I couldn't see the moon anymore.

I let out a gasp as I felt something bump my ankle. I stopped short as it rolled over my shoe. A snake?

No. Too heavy to be a snake.

An animal. *What kind of animal? Were those field rats Skipper told me about actually real?* I shuddered.

"Hey, Mila—" I couldn't hear my voice over the crackle of the cornstalks.

I held my breath and listened to the brush and scrape of Mila's shoes as she darted between the stalks. The crackling grew louder. I couldn't help it. I pictured a gigantic rattlesnake or rat wrapping around my ankle.

The moonlight didn't break through here. I stood in total darkness now, mopping the heavy drops of warm sweat off my forehead and cheeks.

"Hey, Mila—wait up."

No reply. I listened for her footsteps, but I couldn't hear them anymore.

"Mila—?" My voice cracked as I called her name.

Something slid over my shoe again. I glanced down, but it was too dark to see.

"Mila? Hey, come back! Mila? Can you hear me?"

I raised my eyes and searched for the moon. I knew the moon could guide me out of the field. If I turned and walked away from it, I would end up back at the house.

The sky had brightened to charcoal gray. But the moon was not in view.

I spun around and searched in the other direction. Solid sky.

Could I find my way back to the small clearing? No. I was completely turned around now. Surrounded on all sides by tight rows of stalks.

No path. No opening. No clue as to which way I should walk.

"Hey, Mila! Mila!" My shrill voice revealed my fear.

No reply.

Where was she? Didn't she notice I wasn't with her anymore? Why wasn't she coming back for me?

"Ow!" I slapped another fat bug off my forehead.

I was breathing hard. My chest was heaving up and down. My skin tingled as a cold chill swept down my body.

I can't spend all night in this cornfield. I can't! How do I find my way out of here?

And then I had an idea.

I reached into my jeans pocket for my phone.

Not there.

I uttered a frustrated groan and slid my hand into the other pocket.

No. Oh no. The pocket was empty.

I shut my eyes and pictured the phone on the nightstand in my room. I didn't bring it with me.

The first time in my life I really, really needed the phone. And I left it in my room.

A strong burst of wind sent another shiver down my body.

A loud *craaack* made me jump. A stalk cracked in half, and the heavy dry husk thudded against my chest. Another gust of wind sent the stalks swaying back and forth.

Circling me. They're circling me.

A crazy thought. But I had reached total panic mode.

"Mila? Where are you? Mila?" I didn't recognize my own voice.

I held my breath and listened for her footsteps. The only sounds were the steady whine of the wind and the cracking of the stalks.

I cried out as something wrapped around my ankle. For real this time. The gigantic rattlesnake I had imagined?

I kicked my foot up hard. Nearly toppled over backward.

My heart leaped into my throat. I held my breath again and forced myself to calm down.

She'll come back for me. She won't leave me here all night in the cornfield.

My teeth were chattering. Wisps of orange light danced between the tall stalks now. But I couldn't see the moon.

And then I gasped as I heard a whispered voice.

"The corn wants you . . ."

"Huh?" I wasn't sure I had really heard that. Was the wind through the cornstalks playing a joke on me?

"The corn wants you. Stay, Todd. Stay with us."

"Noooo!" A scream burst from my throat. "Mila? Is that you? Mila?"

Silence.

Then: *"Stay with us forever, Todd. The corn is hungry . . . so hungry."*

"Mila? Skipper?" I spun all around. "Not funny!" I screamed. "You're not funny!"

"The corn wants you!"

31

"Noooo!" I screamed again. I grabbed a stalk and slapped it out of my way. Then I took off running.

I ducked my head and stuck my arms out at my sides to brush away the dry stalks. And I ran blindly, not seeing anything at all, except for the deep shadows and the dim flashes of orange light.

I didn't get far.

"Whooooa!" My shoes slid out from under me and I fell. I fell face-forward onto the dry husks, so thick on the ground.

I landed hard on my elbows and knees, and pain shot through my body. The breath whooshed out of me, and I struggled to suck in some air.

I can't stay here. Got to run . . . !

I forced myself to a sitting position. Still gasping for breath, I stood up, my legs shaking.

And powerful hands grabbed my shoulders from behind.

"Skipper!" I screamed. "Get *off* me!"

I twisted free and spun around to face him.

But he wasn't there.

I blinked a few times. My heart thudded in my chest.

Was that a shadow darting into the stalks?

"Hey—Skipper?"

No one there.

No one.

But I could still feel the pressure on my shoulders, still feel the powerful fingers digging into my skin.

"Whoa. Wait."

Squinting into the darkness, I gazed all around. "Are you hiding in the cornstalks?" My voice trembled out in a whisper. "Where are you? Come out. You're not funny. This isn't funny."

I waited, hugging myself, my teeth chattering.

Silence now.

Would they really be this mean to me? Would they really go this far to scare the city kid?

I heard scraping sounds. Soft thuds. Growing louder.

Footsteps crunching toward me.

"Who is it?" I called. "Who is there?"

Mila pushed her way out from between two stalks. Skipper followed her, brushing corn husks away with both hands.

"*There* you are!" Mila cried. She stopped with both hands at her waist and stared at me. "Todd, I was so worried!"

"Why did you wander off?" Skipper swatted a bug off the side of his face. "You got us all scared."

"*You* were scared?" I cried. "How do you think *I* felt?"

"I don't know how we got separated," Mila said. "I searched and searched, but I couldn't find you."

"Why didn't you call?" Skipper demanded.

I slapped my jeans pockets. "I didn't bring my phone."

Skipper rolled his eyes. "Smart move, dude."

"I was so worried, I went back to the house and got Skipper," Mila said. "This was supposed to be a fun night, Todd. You weren't supposed to get lost."

I studied them both. Were they telling the truth?

"The voices," I said. "The whispering voices . . ."

34

They both squinted at me.

"I know you were trying to scare me," I said. "You planned the whole thing, didn't you!"

Mila shook her head. "Of course not," she said. "I wanted you to see the harvest moon, that's all. I didn't want—"

"What about the whispers?" I asked. "About how the corn wants me to stay, how the corn is hungry for me. That was you. I know it was. It *had* to be you."

Mila and Skipper exchanged glances. "Are you totally losing it?" Skipper said.

"What are you talking about?" Mila's eyes grew wide. "Whispers? We don't know anything about any whispers."

She laughed. "Are you trying to scare *us*?"

10

Aunt Clara brushed my hair off my forehead with one hand. "Guess you had quite an adventure, Todd," she said. "Hope you weren't too afraid out there."

"No. It wasn't too bad," I lied.

We were all sitting around the cozy den having bowls of popcorn and tall glasses of hot apple cider. A fire crackled in the brick fireplace against the wall.

"Farms can be scary," Uncle Jake said, setting his glass down on the arm of his chair. "Even an empty cornfield can be frightening if you're not familiar with it."

"I guess," I said.

I didn't want to talk about how frightened I was out there in the field. But I *did* want to talk about the whispers I'd heard.

Skipper and Mila swore they weren't the whisperers. And I kind of believed them. But then, how do you explain those eerie, soft voices?

Thinking about it made me shiver.

"Todd, why are you shaking?" Aunt Clara asked. "Are you cold? Isn't that cider warming you up? Do you want to move away from the window?" She patted the couch cushion beside her. "Here. Come sit by the fire."

"No. I'm okay," I said. I took a long sip of cider. "It's just that . . . well . . . something weird happened out in the cornfield. I . . . uh—"

"We didn't always plant corn in that field," Uncle Jake said. "We started out with soybeans. But it wasn't the moneymaker we thought it would be."

"We love having the corn all summer," Mila added. "This was the first year we grilled it instead of boiling it. And it was awesome."

Skipper shoved a handful of popcorn into his mouth. He was staring hard at me. I couldn't figure out what he was thinking.

"Well . . ." I tried again. "While I was waiting for Mila to find me, I heard these strange whispers. I—"

"Mila wants you to meet her friend tomorrow," Aunt Clara interrupted. "Shameka lives on the closest farm to here."

"But wait till you see it," Mila said. "Their farm is totally modern. It's like sci-fi."

I saw what they were doing. They were deliberately interrupting me. They didn't want to talk about the whispers in the cornfield.

I pulled out my harmonica. I slid it from side to side across my lips. "Would anyone like to hear some blues?" I asked.

"We heard you from upstairs," Skipper said.

Uncle Jake climbed to his feet. "Maybe some other time," he said. He carried his empty popcorn bowl to the kitchen.

Mila yawned. "Yeah. Some other time. It's getting late," she said.

"I can take a hint," I murmured. I tucked the harmonica back into my pocket and made my way upstairs to my attic room.

My suitcase stood open on the floor. I hadn't finished unpacking. I didn't feel sleepy. I think I was still wired from my adventure in the cornfield.

"Guess I'll unpack," I muttered.

The radiator in the corner hissed to life. A burst of wind made the windowpane shake. I glanced out the window. The full moon had faded to yellow and floated high in the sky.

I reached into the suitcase and pulled out the stack of scary books I had brought to read. Remembering the whispers in the cornfield made me shiver. "I don't think I'll be needing these," I said. I shoved the books back into the suitcase and lifted out some sweaters.

My suitcase was nearly empty when I heard the shouts downstairs. I tossed some socks into a dresser drawer and stopped to listen.

An argument? Mila and Skipper were yelling angrily at each other.

What was the argument about? Their voices were muffled behind a closed door. I couldn't make out the words.

I moved closer to the stairs and leaned over the railing, trying to hear better.

I heard Mila call Skipper an idiot.

Then I heard Skipper shout, "You don't know *everything*. You don't know *anything*!"

"You've got to stop! You've got to stop it now!" Mila cried.

More shouting. Something slammed against a wall. Then silence.

The argument had ended. I waited by the stairs to see if it really was over. My brain was spinning. What were they fighting about? It didn't seem like a typical brother-sister argument. They both seemed to be so angry.

Shaking my head, I returned to my room. I pulled more socks from my suitcase and emptied them into a dresser drawer. All unpacked.

I latched the suitcase and dragged it into a corner. Then I stepped over to the dresser to get my pajamas.

I stopped when I realized I wasn't alone.

I turned and blinked when I saw Skipper. He leaned a shoulder against one side of my bedroom doorway. He was so tall, his head came up nearly to the top of the door frame.

He stood there without speaking. Watching me. His eyes narrowed, his expression blank. Just watching me.

"Skipper," I said finally, breaking the silence. "What is it? What's wrong?"

11

Skipper took a few steps into my room. His eyes moved to the window, then back to me.

"What is it?" I repeated. My muscles tensed. Did he come up here to argue with me, too?

He shoved his hands into his pants pockets. "Mila sent me up here to apologize," he muttered.

"Apologize? Wh-why?" I stammered. "Because it was *you* who whispered to me in the cornfield?"

He shook his head. "No. I wasn't there, Todd. I didn't whisper anything to you."

I studied his face. He seemed to be telling the truth. I waited for him to continue.

"Mila told me to apologize for scaring you so much," Skipper said. His cheeks suddenly darkened to red. "All my jokes and teasing . . . well . . . they made you think the farm is a scary place."

The radiator hissed behind me. I dropped down onto the edge of my bed and looked up at Skipper.

"You imagined the whispering," he said.

"Because I put you in a scary mood. I made you think everything here is strange and frightening."

He turned his gaze to the window. His cheeks were still blushing bright red. "I'm really sorry, Todd. I was just having some fun."

"But the whispers were real!" I exclaimed. "It wasn't my imagination, Skipper. I know what I heard."

"It was the wind through the cornstalks," he said. "The same thing happens to my friends and me. It was just the wind, whistling and whispering."

"But—but—" I sputtered.

"The farm is fun," he said. "Don't be afraid." He picked up my grandfather's plastic lighter from my nightstand and twirled it between his fingers. Then he set it back down.

"There's no one around to be scared of," he said. "I mean, the nearest farm is five miles away. So you can just chill and relax, dude."

"Well—" I started.

His eyes flashed. "Have you seen my electric bike? It's seriously awesome. I'll let you ride it. I'll show you how. It's really simple."

"Nice," I said. I stood up. "Thanks for the apology, Skipper."

He nodded and didn't reply. He turned and walked back downstairs.

Well, that was awkward! I told myself.

Nice of him to apologize, I guess. But I don't really believe him.

I changed into my pajamas, turned out the lamp, and climbed under the covers. My head was filled with questions. What were Mila and Skipper fighting about downstairs? Whether or not he should apologize to me? Did she force him to come up to my room? Why?

Minutes dragged on. I couldn't fall asleep.

I picked up the plastic lighter and spun it in my hand for a while. Sometimes it helps to calm me down. But not tonight.

After about an hour, I kicked off the covers and crossed to the window. A white mist had formed around the moon, giving it a ghostly glow. Silvery light washed down over the cornfield.

I pressed my forehead against the glass and gazed down at the swaying stalks. They tilted slowly from side to side, as if moving to music.

I started to yawn. I began to feel hypnotized by the bending corn.

"Oh, wow." I blinked myself alert when I saw something move at the front of the field.

I squinted into the pale light. Someone out there? Someone bent over, crawling?

Yes.

I held my breath—and watched someone crawling out from under the corn.

12

I pressed my forehead against the window glass and stared down. Someone was crawling on hands and knees. Head down.

I blinked several times. Was I dreaming this? Was it just a rabbit or a farm creature? Shadows played over the ground. I squinted harder, but I couldn't see anything clearly.

I started to the stairs. I had to run outside and see who or what it was.

I stopped at my doorway. I didn't want to wake everyone. I didn't want to give them something else to tease me about.

I spun back to my window. I leaned my head out and saw a tree branch. A fat tree branch on an old tree a foot or so to the side of my window.

I opened the window all the way and hoisted myself onto the windowsill. Then I reached out both hands and wrapped them around the limb. I took a deep breath to gather my courage—and pushed myself onto it.

What was I *thinking*?

I'm a city kid. I've never climbed a tree in my life!

And now here I was, hunkered on the rough branch, struggling to keep my balance. My pajama shirt flapped in the chilly breeze. I shivered. The bark felt rough and cold beneath my bare feet.

Slowly, hugging the scratchy trunk tightly, I lowered myself to the ground. My feet landed on wet grass, and I shivered again, and waited for my breathing to slow to normal.

An eerie green light washed over the cornfield. The full moon was now blanketed in a thick curtain of cloud.

I gasped when I heard a groan. And then scratches. Soft thuds of footsteps. The *crunch* of dirt being pushed away.

Hugging myself to stop my shivers, I took a step forward. And then another.

And squinted into the strange light, locking my eyes on the edge of the field, on the bottoms of the swaying stalks.

"Oh nooo." I ducked into the shadows, pressed my back against the tree trunk, and watched figures crawling out, stumbling out, staggering from behind the corn.

Ragged people. Heads down. Hands scrabbling the dirt. One crawled along the side of the field. Another stood up slowly, body bent, hands outstretched, grabbing at the air, reaching . . . reaching for *I don't know what.*

Was I dreaming it? If so, I'd never had a nightmare this frightening, this chilling, and this real.

I clutched the tree trunk and held on as I watched more people stumble out from the field. Dragging their legs, leaning and lurching into the wind, they groaned and grunted as if in pain.

Faces. I couldn't see their faces. They were so bent and half hidden in shadow . . . like an old horror movie in black and white.

I forced myself to breathe. I could feel my heart doing flip-flops in my chest. My throat tightened. I struggled to keep my dinner down.

How many *were* there? I counted at least a dozen. Their heads bobbing as they stumbled out from the stalks. They moved along the field in a single line. Their deep-throated groans rang out over the whir of the cold gusts of wind.

My mouth dropped open in a gasp as they twisted and stumbled into a bright shaft of moonlight. I saw their faces.

And I saw that they were KIDS!

SLAPPY HERE, EVERYONE

Haha. Don't you just love it?

Weird kids crawling around in a cornfield in the middle of the night?

That gives me a warm, fuzzy feeling. Farm life can be so heartwarming. Haha.

Do you think Todd should be scared? *Do* you?

Of *course*, he should be scared! Did you forget this is a *horror* story?

Do you think Todd should bring them cookies and hot chocolate?

I don't think so!

No spoilers here from your wonderful storyteller—me. But I think Todd's problems may just be starting!

13

Too frightened to move, I hugged the tree tightly and tried to stand perfectly still. I held my breath as long as I could and ignored the shivers that rolled down my back.

The wind blew against my pajama shirt. My nose started to itch. I pinched it tightly with my fingers and forced myself not to sneeze.

I watched the strange kids crawl out from the stalks. Rise unsteadily to their feet. Stagger in a strange, painful march along the edge of the field.

Their arms and legs moved stiffly. Their heads bobbed and shook on their shoulders as they made their way, lurching and stumbling.

I waited there, frozen in silent fright, until the last of them disappeared from view. Then I shoved myself away from the tree trunk and went *screaming* into the house.

"Help! Wake up! Wake up! Hurry! Helllllp!"

The words roared from deep in my throat. I

didn't even hear myself. I only knew I had to tell the family what I had seen.

Skipper and Mila appeared first, running barefoot down the stairs. Their hair was tossed from sleep. They shook their heads and blinked themselves awake.

I had to pull Uncle Jake and Aunt Clara from their room. They kept shouting my name, their eyes wide with confusion. "Todd? Todd? Todd? Are you okay?"

"Out back! The field!" I shrieked. "I saw them! I saw them come out!"

Uncle Jake flipped a switch and twin spotlights threw circles of bright light over the front yard. The cornstalks came into sharp focus. The grass under our feet glowed bright green.

"Right there!" I pointed with a trembling finger to the edge of the field. "I . . . I watched them come out! There were so many of them!"

"Whoa. Hold on." Uncle Jake placed his hands on my shoulders. "Slow down, Todd. Take a breath. Come on. Deep breath. Start at the beginning. Tell us what you saw. Slowly, okay?"

I took a deep breath and told them. I started the story at my bedroom window, where I saw the first strange kid crawl out of the corn. And I explained how I made my way down the tree trunk and how I watched them stagger out, one by one. More than a dozen of them. Kids!

I told them the whole story without taking a

breath. They stared at me, listening hard. Their faces were blank. No one interrupted. No one said a word.

"Who are they? What are they? What did I see?" I demanded. "Tell me!"

More silence.

Skipper was the first to speak. "I'm really sorry, Todd. I want to apologize again. I guess I gave you a bad nightmare."

"No—" I started.

Uncle Jake kept his hands on my shoulders. "Calm," he whispered. "Everything is okay, Todd. We're here. We're here to take care of you. You're safe."

Mila shook her head. "I'm sorry, too," she said, brushing her hair out of her eyes. "I should have waited. I should have taken you into the cornfield during *daylight*." She sighed. "But I was so eager for you to see the harvest moon . . ."

"No! No!" I tugged free of Uncle Jake. I spun from one of them to the other, shaking my fists. "You're not *listening* to me! It wasn't a dream! I saw it! I saw them all come crawling out!"

"Todd, listen—" Aunt Clara said softly.

"It was REAL!" I screamed. "Why don't you believe me? It was REAL! They were real! They were like *zombies*!"

My breath caught in my throat. *Zombies.* That was the first time I thought that word. *Zombies.*

Of course. That's what they were.

"They crawled up from the ground," I said. "And staggered and groaned—like *zombies*! Zombie kids!"

Aunt Clara locked her eyes on mine. "You're a sophisticated city kid, Todd. You don't really believe in zombies, do you?"

Skipper laughed. "Do you watch the *Walking Dead* shows on TV?"

I shook my head. "I don't watch that stuff. But I know what I saw, Skipper. I don't have hallucinations, you know? And I almost never have nightmares. You've got to listen to me—"

Aunt Clara shivered and pulled her nightshirt tighter around her. "I'm so sorry you're scared, Todd. The cornfield can look scary at night. But I know things will seem different in the morning."

Uncle Jake rubbed his hands together. "Let's go inside and warm up. We can regroup in the morning and—"

"Wait! Hold on!" I interrupted. "I see something!"

I glimpsed something gray at the edge of the cornfield. "Wait!" I shouted again as I ran over to it. I bent down and lifted it off the ground.

A beat-up shoe.

"I have proof!" I cried. I waved it above my head. "Proof! Here it is!"

I gripped the ragged shoe in both hands. It was covered in mud and smelled terrible, sour and decayed.

"Check it out!" I shouted as I carried it over to them. "Here it is. See? It wasn't a dream. I have proof!"

I shoved the shoe in front of them. They all stared wide-eyed at it. No one said a word.

14

"My old shoe!" Skipper exclaimed. He took it from my hand and studied it. "How did it end up out here?"

Aunt Clara smiled. "Skipper, I remember the day you came home without it. You came hopping into the house on one foot. You never could explain how you managed to lose a shoe!"

Mila rolled her eyes. "Typical Skipper."

"Maybe you walked home through the corn-field," Uncle Jake said. "You were always such an absentminded kid. You probably didn't even realize when the shoe came off."

Skipper shrugged. "Beats me."

I let out a long sigh. I suddenly felt very tired. Sure, I was disappointed that the shoe didn't prove anything.

But why did I need proof? Why didn't anyone in the family believe my story?

I turned and started toward the house. I

knew what the joke would be from now on. *Todd believes in zombies.*

Haha. Funny.

My aunt and uncle stopped me at the stairs. "Todd, are you feeling better? Think you can get to sleep?" Aunt Clara asked.

I shrugged. "I guess."

My uncle smiled. "We're making blueberry pancakes for breakfast tomorrow," he said.

"Nice," I murmured. But that didn't really cheer me up.

I made sure my bedroom window was closed tight. Then I climbed into bed and pulled the covers up to my chin.

I still had chills running down my back. From the cold? Or from the frightening scene I saw? I couldn't tell.

It took a lot of time to fall asleep. And when I did, I had an unpleasant dream.

It started out okay. I dreamed I was back home in New York. I was in my room, and Mom and Dad were in the apartment, too.

Then I went out, and I walked along the street, past shops and restaurants. It all seemed normal at first. But then I realized that the street was empty. No one in sight.

I gazed up and down the sidewalk. And then people came into view.

People walked toward me, and their eyes were wide and solid white. I cried out because

I realized they were staggering and lurching and stumbling. They stretched their hands out, their arms stiff, as if reaching for me, grabbing for me.

Zombies.

I woke up with a silent scream. My face was drenched in a cold sweat.

I gazed all around the room, making sure it was just a dream. Then I slid out from under the covers and walked on shaky legs to the window.

A red sun was just coming up. I could tell there was no breeze. The dry brown cornstalks stood straight up at attention.

I stepped out of my room and listened. Silence. Everyone was still asleep.

I woke up with one idea in my head. I wanted to find proof. I needed to make everyone believe me.

And I had to know the truth.

I pulled on jeans and a hoodie and quietly tiptoed down the stairs. I carefully clicked the front door closed behind me.

The air still carried a chill from the night before. The grass leading up to the cornfield sparkled in the morning dew, and my shoes sank into the wet ground.

I stopped at the edge of the field. The stalks rose above me, like a wall.

What exactly did I hope to find?

I didn't know.

But I knew there had to be some clue.

Footprints, maybe. Or something those strange, frightening kids had dropped.

I took a deep breath and prepared to step into the rows of stalks. I jumped back when a fat brown squirrel darted out and leaped over my shoes. Its tail raised high, it ran along the edge of the field. Then disappeared back into the stalks.

I silently scolded myself. *It isn't helpful to be afraid of a squirrel, Todd.*

But, of course, I was afraid.

Were those zombie kids back in the cornfield? Had they seen me? Were they waiting for me?

Todd—you're a New Yorker, I told myself. *You're not afraid of a cornfield. You're not afraid of* anything*!*

I shoved two stalks out of my way and stepped into the field. I made my way down one row, then turned and walked the next. I kept my eyes on the ground. My shoes crunched over the dead leaves and husks.

The sun rose higher in the morning sky, and the air grew warmer. I mopped my forehead with the sleeve of my hoodie.

I kept the sun in front of me. That way, I couldn't get lost again. If I wanted to leave the cornfield, all I had to do was turn my back to the sun.

I told myself I was too clever to be afraid. But why was my heart pounding like a bass drum?

I tapped the plastic lighter in my jeans pocket. Luck. Good luck.

I thought it might take a while to find the proof I was searching for. But it didn't take long at all.

I stopped and squinted at the ground between stalks. I bent down to get a closer look.

Yes. Yes. I had definitely found something.

15

Large openings in the ground.

I squatted down and could see that the dirt had been shoved aside around them.

How many were there?

Keeping low to the ground, I pressed myself between the stalks. "Whew." I counted at least a dozen openings in the dirt.

A dozen *graves*?

I stared at the dirt piled up at the edge of each hole.

Had those kids climbed up from under the dirt? Pushed up from their graves? And then staggered out of the cornfield?

It was insane. The whole idea. Impossible.

But here I was, staring at the piles of dirt, the open graves.

Hey, I'm a horror fan. I love scary stuff.

But this felt very different. It wasn't fun. It was too *real*.

At least now I had my proof.

The family couldn't laugh at me now. They couldn't say I had a bad nightmare last night.

They had to believe me.

Brushing dirt off the knees of my jeans, I went running back to the house. "Hey—!" I called as I burst into the kitchen.

Uncle Jake already had a skillet of pancake batter on the stove. Skipper and Mila sat at the table in their pajamas. Aunt Clara stood by the sink, a mug of coffee between her hands.

"Where've *you* been?" Uncle Jake asked.

"I found my proof," I said. "Come with me. Hurry. You have to believe me now."

"Not now," my uncle said. "You see I have pancakes on the stove."

Skipper and Mila groaned. "Give it a rest, Todd. It's too early for that zombie stuff."

"But—but—" I sputtered. "I have to show you what I found. I—"

"Why don't you just *tell* us?" Aunt Clara said. She took a long sip of coffee. "You don't have to show us right now. Just tell us what you found."

"Okay, okay," I said. I took a breath. "I found all these holes in the cornfield. Lots of holes in the ground. With dirt piled up on the sides."

Uncle Jake shook his head. "Todd, listen—"

"They weren't old," I said. "The holes are fresh. They have to be open graves. There are so many of them, you won't believe it."

Uncle Jake lifted the pan off the stove and

flipped the pancakes. "Perfect," he muttered.

"Did you hear what I said?" I cried. My voice burst out high and shrill.

"Raccoons," Skipper said. He rubbed his fork and knife together.

Mila nodded. "Raccoons," she echoed. "There are more and more of them every year."

"Excuse me?" I cried. I took a few steps toward the table.

"Mila is right," Aunt Clara said. "The raccoons are a real problem here, Todd. Their population grows every year."

"But—" I started.

"When fall comes," Uncle Jake said, "gangs of them overrun the cornfields. They are looking for any scraps of food they can find."

He turned off the stove burner and slid the stack of pancakes onto a big platter. "And they dig themselves beds to sleep in," he said.

I swallowed. "Beds? You mean—"

Uncle Jake nodded. "Those holes you saw . . . they're raccoon beds."

I shut my eyes. My brain was spinning.

Were they telling the truth? I'd never heard of raccoon beds.

Aunt Clara slid a chair out from the table. "Take that stunned look off your face, Todd, and sit down," she said. "You don't want your pancakes to get cold."

I dropped into the chair and scraped it up to

the table. "You're probably all starting to think I'm seriously weird," I said.

"Yes, we do," Skipper said. "Seriously weird."

Everyone laughed.

Everyone but me.

I knew what I saw the night before.

And I knew I had to prove it to them.

But how?

16

Aunt Clara drove Mila and me to Mila's friend's house. We passed more empty cornfields, some narrow creeks, and vast stretches of woods. Shameka lived in the nearest farmhouse, about five miles away.

She was waiting for us on the back porch as our truck crackled up the gravel driveway. She had short black hair and light brown skin. She waved and came trotting toward us. I laughed at her T-shirt. It had an arrow pointing up at her face that read *I'm with ME*.

Grinning, she swung open the truck door, grabbed my hand, and yanked me to the ground so hard I nearly fell over. "Hi, City Kid!" she exclaimed. "Was that your first time in a truck?" She raised her phone. "Shall we take a selfie to send to Mom?"

I rolled my eyes. "Are you going to give me a tough time, too?" I asked.

She laughed. She was nearly a foot shorter than

me. But she had a deep-throated laugh that rang in the air. "No way, Todd. I won't make fun of you for being a city kid. Actually, I'm from Brooklyn."

"You're joking," I said. "Where?"

"Flatbush."

"My grandmother was born in Flatbush," I said.

Mila gave Shameka a push toward the house. "This is a thrilling conversation," she said. "I may die from the excitement."

Shameka winked at me. "She's totally jealous."

"How did you end up out here in Moose Hollow?" I asked.

"My dad made a wrong turn in Kenosha!" she exclaimed.

We both laughed.

"You and Todd have the same sense of humor," Mila said. "Bad."

Shameka led us through the back door. The air was warm in the kitchen and smelled sweet. "We had cinnamon rolls for breakfast," Shameka said. "Sorry I forgot to save you one."

The kitchen looked modern and bright. Little spotlights shone down from the ceiling. The floor was red tile, and the cabinets were all painted bright yellow. "Mom is an artist, and she likes bright colors," Shameka explained.

"The whole house is pretty awesome," Mila said. "And wait till you see their chicken coop. It's state-of-the-art."

"You'll want to live in it," Shameka said.

"I like my attic room at Mila's," I said. "It's like my own little world."

"Mila *told* me you were weird," Shameka said.

"I did not!" Mila protested.

Shameka led us into a large den with bright green leather couches, a red leather armchair, and throw pillows of all colors scattered everywhere. "We're having brats for lunch," she said. "Todd needs the whole Wisconsin thing, right?"

Mila pulled two guitars from behind one of the couches. She handed one to Shameka. They sat down across from each other and started to tune them.

I dropped down onto a big throw pillow and leaned my back against the wall. A gray cat with bright green eyes appeared from out of nowhere and rubbed its back against my leg.

"She's very friendly," Shameka said. "But she'll bite you if she decides she doesn't like you."

"Thanks for the warning," I said. The cat purred and rubbed its back some more.

Mila and Shameka began to play their guitars. A fast country rhythm. "Mila and I have a band," Shameka said.

I pulled out my harmonica and joined in.

They both stopped playing at once.

I lowered the harmonica to my lap. "What's wrong?"

"Did you ever take lessons on that thing?" Shameka asked.

I shook my head. "No."

"I thought so," she said.

"Maybe you should have it tuned," Mila chimed in.

"You don't tune a harmonica," I said. "There's nothing to tune."

"Maybe you should try the saxophone," Shameka said. And they both laughed.

I slapped the harmonica against my palm. "Okay. I get it," I murmured. "You don't like my playing."

"You probably have other talents," Shameka said.

"I can rehearse," I said. "Really. I'm not that bad. Can't I be in your band? If I work at it?"

They stared at me.

"That's my dream," I said. "To be in a band."

"Keep dreaming," Shameka said. And they both laughed again.

I let out a growl and jammed the harmonica back into my pocket. "You two are a riot," I muttered.

They ignored me and played some more. I tried to pet the cat, but she spun away and strutted out of the den with her tail in the air.

I shifted my weight on the big pillow. "What is your band called?" I asked.

"Canned Meat," Mila said.

I blinked. "Huh? Canned Meat? Why Canned Meat?"

Both girls giggled in reply.

"No. Seriously," I said. "Why Canned Meat?"

They giggled again. Then Shameka said, "Maybe you'll soon find out."

17

Shameka's chicken coop was as amazing as the girls had said. It was white and bright and clean. I was ready to hold my nose. But the air was fresh and sweet.

Shameka pointed to what looked like a tunnel beneath the chicken roosts. "See? It's a built-in conveyor belt," she explained. "The eggs roll down to the end of each row. We don't need any-one to pick them up."

"What are those fluffy white chickens?" I asked.

"Those are Silkies," Shameka said. "Aren't they the cutest? We have a few of them. But most of these chickens are New Hampshire Reds."

"You'd be amazed how much personality a chicken has," Mila said.

"Yes, I would," I replied. "The only chickens I've ever met were fried or roasted."

They both rolled their eyes.

We walked up and down the rows. Chickens

clucked and pecked seed and strutted. I guess that's what they mostly do.

At the end of a row, Shameka suddenly stopped and turned to Mila. A thoughtful look crossed her face. "Hey, Mila," she said. "Did you tell Todd about what happened to that fifth-grade class from Ann Arbor?"

To my surprise, Mila gasped. Her expression turned angry. "Shameka—*shut up!*" she cried. "I mean it. *Shut up!*"

18

I followed them out of the chicken coop. The afternoon sun was high in a pale blue sky. Puffy white clouds floated low over the roof of the farmhouse.

"You really should tell Todd," Shameka insisted.

Mila turned to face her. "No way! Why should I tell him?" She shook her head. "I don't believe you're doing this. Why did you even bring it up?"

I stepped between them. "Stop shouting at each other," I said. "You really have no choice now. You have to tell me whatever it is."

Mila balled up her fists and shook them at Shameka. Shameka stood her ground, staring back at her.

"Why don't you want to tell me?" I asked.

I followed them to the back porch. Two wooden porch swings faced each other. I sat down. They took the one across from me.

"I didn't want to tell you," Mila said, "because

you just got here. I didn't want to scare you, that's all."

I laughed. "Are you kidding me? Everyone has been trying to scare me nonstop!"

"This is serious," Mila insisted.

Shameka tucked her legs beneath her. "I think Todd needs to know," she said softly. "He's going to find out sooner or later."

"Just shut up," Mila snapped. "I mean it—"

"Stop arguing," I said. I turned to Shameka. "You started it. So go ahead. Tell me. What's the big secret?"

They glared at each other. Mila was definitely angry. She sighed and rolled her eyes. "Okay, okay," she said. "Here goes. A true story, Todd."

I leaned forward and swung gently back and forth. The swing made a soft squeaking sound with each move.

"It took place a few years back," Mila started. "A class of fifth graders from Michigan were on a bus, and they came through here. Some kind of field trip, I guess."

"Their bus stopped at Mila's farm," Shameka said. "It parked in front of the cornfield. The kids thought it would be fun to explore it. I don't think they were farm kids."

"It was summer, and the corn was high and thick," Mila said. "The whole class went into the cornfield with their teacher, and . . ."

She hesitated. She glanced at Shameka.

"And they were never seen again!" Shameka said breathlessly.

Both girls stared wide-eyed at me. No one moved. They were waiting to see my reaction.

I gazed at one, then the other.

Then I burst out laughing.

Mila grabbed my arm. "Todd, what's wrong with you? Didn't you hear what we just said? The kids were never seen again."

Shameka squinted hard at me. "How can you laugh at that?"

"Easy," I said. "You farm people will do *anything* to try to scare a city dude."

"You're wrong. We're telling the truth," Shameka insisted.

"Ha," I said. "Sorry, but it's not going to work on me. I know exactly what happened here."

They both crossed their arms in front of them and frowned at me.

"Mila knew I saw something weird out in the cornfield," I explained. "I thought it was kids crawling out from the corn. But maybe I was wrong. It was my first night, and I was really tired. Maybe I *did* dream it. Maybe my imagination went berserk . . ."

They didn't move, listening to my explanation.

I continued, "So Mila called you up, Shameka, and she said, 'Here's a trick we can play on Todd. He thinks he saw kids in the cornfield. So let's make up a story and tell him a class of fifth graders disappeared in the field and never came out. Todd will be shaking. It will totally creep him out.'"

"That's not true!" both girls screamed at once.

I laughed again. "I don't scare so easy. I'm a New Yorker. We have *rats* bigger than those chickens!"

Mila gritted her teeth. "Listen to us, Todd. There's more. We haven't finished the story."

"There's something else you need to know," Shameka said. "Something terrible. You see—"

"Lunchtime!" a voice interrupted.

Shameka's mom appeared on the porch. "Come on. Come get your lunch before it gets cold."

I jumped up and followed the two girls into the kitchen. What did they want to tell me? What was the rest of their made-up story? They never finished, so I knew I was right. They were just trying to scare me.

Later that day, an hour before dinner, Skipper took me for a ride on the back of his electric bike. We rode down the gravel driveway, away from the farm, and onto the county road.

There were no cars in sight. Skipper gunned it, and it felt like we were zooming at one hundred miles an hour.

The strangest thing about the bike? It was completely silent.

The cool air whipped my cheeks as the late-afternoon sun lowered behind the trees. Leaves had started to turn yellow and brown. It didn't feel like summer anymore.

Back home, Skipper picked up a softball in the yard, and we started to toss it back and forth along the edge of the cornfield. "I thought I might get serious about playing baseball," he told me. "But I messed up my knee in sixth grade."

"That's bad news," I said.

He scrunched up his face. "Can you imagine? I was twelve and my whole career was over." He threw the ball high, over my head. "Oh. Sorry."

I chased it across the grass and tossed it back to him.

"Do you play any sports?" he asked.

"Not really," I said. "Well . . . I take tennis lessons. That's about it."

We threw the ball in silence for a while. Then he asked, "Are you tense about starting school on Monday?"

I shrugged. "A little."

"It will be different from back in New York," he said, then snickered. "You will probably be shocked at how small the school is."

I nodded. "*Everything* is different here." I caught the ball low and held on to it.

"Can I ask you something?"

74

"For sure," he said. He walked closer. "What's up?"

I told him the story Shameka and Mila told me about the fifth-grade class from Michigan going into the cornfield. I thought they had made it up, but I just wanted to make sure. "They said those kids were never seen again." I locked my eyes on Skipper's. "Is that story true?"

He shook his head. "Of course not. No way," he said. He ran a hand through his long hair. "I don't believe it," he murmured. "Mila tells me to stop scaring you. Then she goes ahead and tells you that crazy story."

I opened my mouth to reply. But I stopped when I heard a sound. From the cornfield.

Howls. Long and low. Rising and falling.

Human-sounding howls ringing out from deep in the field.

My mouth dropped open.

A gust of wind seemed to carry the howls and swirl them all around me.

I covered my ears and turned to Skipper.

He was watching me. "Farm cats," he said. "Feral cats. They live in the wild. In the cornfield. They howl like that all the time."

20

First day of school.

Yes. Skipper was right. It was a lot smaller than P.S. 196 in Forest Hills. Mila and I are in fifth grade, and Skipper is in eighth. But we were in the same building.

It was about a twenty-minute drive from the farm. Aunt Clara dropped us off in front of the square, redbrick school. It looked more like a house than a school to me.

I could see a playground for little kids on one side. And a grassy soccer field stretching along the other side. Behind the school, a forest with a border of tall trees made a high wall.

I waved to Aunt Clara as she pulled the truck away from the school. And I followed Mila and Skipper up the stairs to the front entrance.

Mila gave me a gentle shove. "Don't look so nervous, Todd."

"You're *supposed* to be nervous on the first day of school," I said.

"You definitely *should* be nervous," Skipper said. "It's a new school, new teacher, and you don't know anyone. You don't even know where the bathroom is!"

"Shut up, Skipper!" Mila snapped. "You're not funny." She turned to me. "No worries. I'll show you around. It isn't too hard."

A gray-haired woman in a dark blue skirt and a pale blue sweater opened the glass door for us. She had bright green eyes behind her square eyeglasses. Her face was pale except for the dark lipstick on her smiling mouth.

She nodded to Mila and Skipper, then turned her smile on me. "You must be Todd," she said. "I'm Mrs. Bane, the principal." She had a smooth, young voice. "Welcome to Moose Hollow School. I've heard a lot about you."

"Really?" I said. *Awkward.* I never know what to say when someone says that.

"Todd is nervous," Skipper said. "You know. New school."

Why did he tell her that? Just to embarrass me?

Mrs. Bane's smile grew wider. "I'm sure everyone will make you feel at home." She turned to Mila. "Will you show Todd to his locker and then to Miss Opperman's classroom?"

The principal glanced at the large watch on her wrist. "Please scoot. We really need to hurry now."

Mrs. Bane turned to some kids who were talking by the wall of lockers. "Classrooms, people!" she called. "Hurry. No loitering in the hall. Scoot!"

Mila put a hand on my shoulder and pushed me down the hall. "This way. I'll show you. Here's your locker."

"What's the big hurry?" I asked. "Why is she making everyone rush? It's early."

Mila didn't answer.

I shoved my backpack into the locker. Then I hurried to catch up to her.

At the end of the hall, we turned a corner. She stopped in front of a closed classroom door. Room 4-A.

"This is your room," Mila said. She pointed. "My class is near the front."

"Huh?" I blinked. "But I thought we'd be in the same class."

She shook her head. "Hurry. Go in. I'll see you later."

I started to ask her again. But she was already running down the hall toward her room, her shoes banging on the tile floor.

"Well . . . here goes," I muttered. I took a deep breath and pulled open the door.

21

"Are you Todd?" Miss Opperman jumped up from her desk chair. She was fairly young and on the short side, with black hair and dark eyes. Her slacks were black, but she wore a bright purple-and-white Moose Hollow sweatshirt.

"Come in. Please hurry." She turned to the class. I saw about a dozen kids, already sitting behind their desks. "Hey, everyone. This is Todd. He's our only new student this year."

They all studied me as if I was some kind of science lab experiment.

"Tell everyone where you are from, Todd," the teacher said.

"Queens, New York," I said.

"Cool," a boy said from the back of the room. No one else made a sound.

"How many of you have ever been to New York?" Miss Opperman asked.

Two hands went up.

"I saved you a desk by the window," the teacher said, pointing.

I made my way to the desk and slid into it. I wondered when everyone would stop watching me like I was some kind of alien invader.

Someone had scratched the word *bored* into the wooden desktop. Outside the window, I could see the trees in the forest, their leaves already brown and yellow.

I gazed around the room. It was strange seeing all new faces. Kids I didn't know. Like starting life all over again, only more awkward.

You can do this, Todd, I told myself.

You're pretty smart. You're not shy. You know how to get along with kids.

"Hey." The boy next to me tapped my desktop.

I turned. He had short blond hair and a pale, round face dotted with freckles. He wore a red T-shirt with the bright green face of the Hulk bursting across the front.

"My family went to New York once," he said. "It was fun."

I nodded. "I don't live in Manhattan. I live across the river."

He narrowed his blue eyes at me. "How come you came here?"

I shrugged. "It's a long story. What's your name?"

"Owen. Do you play *Minecraft*?"

"Yeah. I'm into it," I said.

"Maybe someday after school—" he started, taking a notebook from his backpack.

I jumped to my feet. I suddenly realized I'd shoved my backpack, with my notebook in it, into my locker near the front entrance.

I started to ask Miss Opperman if I could go get it. But she was writing something on the chalkboard, and her back was turned.

I made my way along the wall, then darted out of the room. No one in the hall. I felt turned-around for a moment. Then I remembered the way to the front, where the lockers were.

My footsteps echoed in the empty hall. My locker was number 103, right across from the glass entrance door. Some of the lockers had padlocks, but mine didn't.

I pulled open the locker door and reached down for my backpack. But then I stopped.

Through the door, I saw a bus pull up to the front of the school. I squinted into the sun's reflection on the glass.

I could see that it wasn't a typical school bus. It was painted gray. A lot of the paint had cracked away. I saw big rust spots on the side. The front fender was crumpled, caved in.

I tried to see inside. But the windows were solid black.

"Weird," I muttered to myself.

But then things got weirder.

The bus door swung open. I watched as a kid stepped out. His head was lowered. A black hood hung loosely over his head. One sleeve of his hoodie was missing.

His dark pants were torn at the knees and the leg bottoms were ragged. His shoes were caked with mud.

He slouched toward the school building. And then another kid appeared in the bus doorway.

I squinted hard, confused by the strange sight. *Who are these kids?*

I didn't have time to think about it. A hand grabbed my shoulder. Tightened its grip. Spun me around.

Mrs. Bane!

"Todd—what are you *doing* out here?" she shrieked. "Get away from the door! Hurry! Get back to your classroom—NOW!"

I swiped my backpack off the locker floor, whirled away, and went running down the hall. I don't think I even closed the locker door.

What is going on here?

My head spun. My shoulder throbbed from the principal's strong grip. Nearly to my classroom, I stopped to catch my breath.

I could hear voices behind me. The voices of the kids who had just arrived.

I tried to make out their words. But their voices were low and growly. Too rough to be kids' voices.

My heartbeats were pounding. But I had to get a better look at those kids.

Keeping against the wall, I turned and crept halfway back. "Oh, wow," I muttered as I saw a bunch of them moving into a classroom.

Some were staggering. Dragging their legs as they stumbled through the open door. Some wore hoods that completely covered their faces. Others had their heads down as they shuffled into the class.

"Todd?"

I turned and saw Miss Opperman waving frantically to me from her classroom door. I took a deep breath and trotted over to her.

"I'm waiting for you," she said. "You know you can't just jump up and leave class whenever you feel like it."

"I . . . had to get my backpack," I stammered. I held it up in front of her as if proving it to her.

"But you shouldn't be out of the room," she repeated. She put a hand on the back of my neck and guided me gently to the door.

"Uh . . . wait," I said. "Can you tell me—?"

"No," she interrupted. "I can't."

"But—but—"

She kept her hand on my neck until I started down the aisle to my desk. Once again, I could feel all eyes on me.

I slumped into my chair. Beside me, Owen kept his eyes focused on his textbook and avoided me.

"I just saw something strange," I murmured. I thought that might make him turn around. But he didn't.

I can't tell you what anyone talked about the rest of the morning. I completely zoned out. I couldn't stop thinking about those ragged, growling kids climbing off that beat-up, rusted school bus and staggering into the school.

Were they the same kids who crawled out from the corn and marched along the field? Were they different kids? Was the whole town filled with zombie kids?

Chill after chill ran down my back. I couldn't erase their ugly faces and twisted bodies from my mind.

One thought kept repeating and repeating: *Zombies don't go to school.*

Right?

Right?

I searched for Mila and Shameka at lunch and couldn't find them.

The lunchroom was small, with three long picnic tables taking up most of the room. Kids were jammed on the benches, talking loudly, laughing, and eating lunches from home.

At the back table, a dark-haired boy jumped to his feet and tossed a crushed juice can at a boy across the room. It bounced off the kid's head, and everybody laughed and cheered.

I recognized some of the kids from my class. But no sign of Mila and Shameka.

"Weird," I muttered. I knew they couldn't go home for lunch. The school stood all by itself, surrounded by miles of farm fields and woods.

I gobbled down the sandwich Aunt Clara had packed for me. Then I hurried back into the hall to continue my search.

The halls were quiet and empty, except for a couple of teachers who leaned against some lockers and were laughing quietly about something. They didn't turn around when I passed by.

The classroom doors were all open. I peeked into each class, hoping to find Mila and Shameka. But everyone seemed to be at lunch.

"Whoa." I stopped. One door near the front of the school was shut. The words ROOM 5-Z were stenciled in black on the door.

I heard low voices inside. Shuffling footsteps. A chair scraped on the floor. Someone coughed, a loud, rough cough.

I moved closer to the door. I heard a woman say, "Can we continue our talk now?"

I heard mumbled replies.

Someone touched my shoulder and I jumped.

I spun around to see Owen gazing at me intently. "Hey—!" I started.

He brought his freckled face close to mine, and whispered, "Better move on, Todd. If you don't bother them, they won't bother you."

SLAPPY HERE, EVERYONE

I don't know what Todd is upset about. *Every* school has its weirdos—right?

In your school, it's probably YOU! Hahaha.

You'd better listen to Owen, Todd. You might be dying to learn the truth about them—but you don't want to be DYING for real! Haha.

I hope Todd enjoys fifth grade. At the rate he's going, he may be there *forever*! Hahaha.

23

Mila went to Shameka's house after school, and I didn't see her until dinnertime. Uncle Jake served what he called his "famous Sloppy Joe" sandwiches, with potato salad.

"Bet you don't have these in New York," he said, dropping a bun overstuffed with hamburger meat and tomato sauce on my plate.

"You'd win that bet," I said.

Skipper had already eaten a whole sandwich. He had orange sauce dripping down his chin. He hummed as he ate, obviously enjoying it.

I raised my gaze to Mila, who sat across the table from me. "Where were you and Shameka at lunchtime?" I asked. "I looked for you both."

She swallowed some sandwich, then smiled. "Shameka and I have a secret lunch place."

"Why didn't you tell me?" I asked. "I searched—"

"How was your first day at school?" Aunt Clara interrupted.

"Not too bad," I said, still watching Mila. "Except I saw these weird kids. They got off a bus and—"

"I made the sauce a little spicy this time," Uncle Jake interrupted. "What do you think?"

"I like it," Skipper said. He was almost finished with his second sandwich. "Tangy."

"Ooh, good word!" Mila teased him.

"Don't make fun," Uncle Jake scolded her. "It *is* a good word. It's the *perfect* word."

I pounded the table with my fist. "Why won't you let me talk?" I cried. "Why don't you want to talk about these strange kids? They were in school today and—"

"Please, Todd—lower your voice," Uncle Jake said.

"Let's have a pleasant dinner," Aunt Clara said, helping herself to more potato salad. "We can talk about unpleasant things later."

"Unpleasant?" I said. My voice came out higher than I'd planned. "Is that what you call it? A bunch of zombie kids who come to school and—"

I heard a CRASH.

I looked up and saw a puddle of water spreading over the table. Mila had spilled her water glass.

"Oh! Sorry!" She began mopping up the water with her napkin.

Did she knock her glass over on purpose? To stop me from talking about the zombie kids?

Aunt Clara brought paper towels from the kitchen. Mila kept apologizing as she cleaned up the spill.

I didn't want to give up. When everyone was seated again, I said, "I was telling you about the zombie kids—"

"There's no such thing as zombies," Mila said. "I saw those scary books you brought, Todd. Maybe you've been reading too many of them. Maybe—"

Aunt Clara raised both hands to quiet us. "Let's all stay calm and enjoy these great sandwiches."

And so we did. We stayed calm and we didn't talk about the zombie kids, and we acted as if everything was perfectly normal and okay.

But I was too upset to enjoy the Sloppy Joes. I wanted answers. I wanted to know the truth.

I hoped I could talk to Skipper about everything after dinner. But he jumped up from the table and said he had to meet a friend. A few seconds later, I watched him speed away on his electric bike.

Mila hurried to her room and closed the door.

Aunt Clara was on cleanup duty. She washed the dishes, and I dried.

When we were nearly finished, she turned off the water and pulled me to the side of the sink. She glanced around, as if making sure we were alone. "Let me tell you something, Todd," she said. Her voice was just above a whisper.

I waited for her to continue.

Her eyes locked on mine. "We want you to enjoy yourself here," she said. "Don't worry about things. If you see something that is troubling to you ... just remember we are here to take care of you."

"But—" I started.

She pressed her hand over my mouth. Her hand was still hot and damp from the dishwater. "Sshhh." After a few seconds, she pulled it away.

"Okay," she said. "I'll tell you just one thing about your school. I'm just going to tell you one thing. Then, no questions."

I nodded. "Okay. No questions."

She lowered her voice even more. "Listen carefully ..."

24

Aunt Clara's voice stayed just above a whisper. "Here, every kid has to go to school. It's the law."

I stared at her and waited for her to say more. But she didn't.

"I . . . don't understand," I said finally.

She shrugged. "You agreed. No questions."

"But . . . why are you telling me about the law?" I demanded.

"No questions. That's a question," she replied. She turned back to the sink. "Just a few glasses left. I'll finish up. You can go to your room."

My head was spinning. Why was she being so mysterious? Why was she telling me about a state law?

I glanced out the kitchen window. A red evening sun was low in the purple sky. "Think I'll take a walk," I said. "You know. Get some exercise."

I wanted to walk and think and try to figure things out. But I didn't say that.

Uncle Jake was still at the dining room table,

sifting through a stack of papers. I gave him a wave as I passed by and stepped outside.

The evening air felt cool against my cheeks. No breeze at all. The cornstalks in the field stood tall, at attention.

I crossed the yard and started to walk along the edge of the cornfield. *I need to chill,* I told myself. My brain was buzzing like a swarm of insects was swirling inside it.

The field was covered in shadow. My shoes sank into the soft ground as I walked along the edge. I suddenly felt as if I was on Mars or the moon or some other planet. The only person here. All alone in this strange, nearly silent land.

I stopped when I realized I wasn't alone.

Two large rabbits stood frozen on their hind legs a few feet up ahead. Their ears stood straight up. They were as still as statues, dark eyes gleaming in the twilight.

I stood as still as they did and stared back at them. *Who will blink first?*

Without warning, they turned at the same time and darted into the tall stalks.

Todd, you're not in New York anymore, I told myself.

And then: *You don't have zombie kids in your neighborhood.*

And then: *Zombies don't go to school.*

And then thought after thought about field rats and snakes and raccoon beds and zombies, all crashing together in my mind, like bumper cars at a carnival, bouncing into one another, sending one another spinning crazily out of control.

How far had I walked?

I hadn't paid any attention. And now, squinting into the dim evening light, the top of the moon floating above the horizon, I realized I'd walked far.

The end of the cornfield lay just up ahead. I'd walked the entire length of the field. How many acres? I'd have to ask my aunt or uncle.

A chill tightened the muscles in my neck. The evening air had turned colder.

I started to turn back—when I saw something up ahead. A long gray object at the very far end of the field.

I took a few steps closer, squinting into the grayness.

"Huh?" I gasped when I recognized it.

The bus. The bent and beat-up school bus. Parked right up against the wall of empty stalks.

Todd—run!

Yes. My first thought was to run. Get away from that bus before anyone saw me.

But something held me there. Something told me this might be my chance to solve the mystery.

I took a deep breath and started to walk to the bus.

25

A cold gust of wind blew against my face, as if trying to push me away. But I lowered my head and kept walking toward the bus.

The cornstalks came to life and began swaying from side to side, crackling like snapping bones. I heard the flapping of wings overhead. A night-hawk, I guessed.

I didn't take my eyes off the bus. It was parked at a slant, tilting toward the field.

Halfway there, I stopped. Were those voices I heard? Low voices in the cornfield? Or just the wind through the dry husks?

No. They were human voices. I cupped a hand over one ear, trying to make out the words. What were they saying?

I didn't see anyone. But I could hear their voices. Soft and mumbled. Murmured words I couldn't hear clearly. Were they coming from the bus?

I pictured those broken, bent kids crawling out

from under the stalks. And saw those same eerie figures staggering and stumbling into Room 5-Z at school.

I knew I should run.

But I couldn't. I couldn't leave. I had to know the truth.

I'm a New Yorker. I'm not afraid of anything.

Not a totally convincing thought. But it helped a little as I started to walk again.

My shoes crunched on dead leaves and corn husks as I stepped to the side of the bus. The windows were solid black. The door hung open.

"Hey—" I tried to call out. But my voice escaped in a hoarse whisper. I moved up to the open bus door. "Hey—anyone in there?"

Silence except for the rustle of the stalks in the field behind me.

"C-can anyone hear me?" I stammered. "Anyone on the bus?"

No answer.

I grabbed the edge of the door and pulled myself to the first step.

Should I risk climbing inside?

Of *course* I shouldn't. But I had to.

I had to know what was happening here. What was this all about?

I ducked my head and pulled myself into the darkened bus.

26

"Oh, wow."

I started to choke from the putrid smell. Like ten-year-old garbage left to rot. My eyes started to water. I shut them tight and held my breath.

The bus floor creaked under my shoes as I took a few steps into the aisle. I slid my phone from my jeans pocket and clicked on the flashlight.

In the shaky white light, the inside of the bus looked like a garbage pit. Stuffing spilled from the torn and broken seats. A pile of rotting clothes covered two seats. Torn T-shirts and shorts and pants covered in stains.

Flies buzzed at the back of the bus. I stopped halfway there. I didn't want to see what they were buzzing over.

My light stopped at a brown paper bag on the seat next to me. I tore it open and found some kind of sandwich. Were those worms poking in and out of the moldy bread? Yes.

I dropped the bag and covered my mouth, struggling to keep my dinner down.

Did those kids really ride in this disgusting, horrifying bus to school?

I held my breath, but it didn't keep the heavy, sour odor from invading my nose.

"I have to get out of here." My heart began to pound.

I turned to the front. Took a step.

"Whoooa." I stumbled over something. Fell onto my knees on the sticky bus floor.

What did I trip over?

I slid the light from my phone in front of me. A shoe. A shoe left in the aisle.

Oh, wait. Oh no. Oh no.

There's a foot in the shoe!

A scream escaped my throat. I shut my eyes tight, trying to unsee what I had just seen.

Blindly, I stumbled to the front and leaped off the bus. Pain shot up my legs as I landed hard on the ground. Ignoring it, I started to run away.

I stopped short when I saw something moving in the cornfield.

The tall stalks leaned to the side, crackling loudly. And then I saw kids lurching out from between them.

Grunting and muttering in low growls, they slid between the stalks and dragged themselves onto the grassy field.

"Ohhh." My mouth dropped open and my eyes

bulged as I saw them so close. I could see their twisted faces, jagged mouths, cracked skin, and blank, unseeing eyes.

Their bodies were bent and stiff and moved awkwardly, as if they had little control of their muscles. Their mouths hung open. Even in the dim light, I could see that several of them had no teeth.

Their bodies brushed the dry stalks as they moved toward me. Frozen in terror, I watched, trembling, as they formed a tight line facing me.

Run.

The word rang in my mind but didn't seem to have any meaning.

And then, without any thought, I forced myself to stop staring at them. I whirled around, so hard I nearly fell. And then took a step and another . . . until I was running.

Running hard without glancing back.

I could hear them coming after me. Hear their ragged footsteps, their mutterings, and their growls.

I struggled to run faster. My legs ached and throbbed and I gasped for each breath.

I didn't get far.

I cried out as something hit me hard. Hit the back of my head.

I fell forward. Hit the ground on my elbows and knees.

Caught.

27

I dropped onto my stomach, breathing in short gasps. Over my wheezing breaths, I could hear their low growls. I shut my eyes and waited for them to pounce.

Waited.

I opened my eyes, raised my head, and glanced back.

"Huh?" I gasped when I realized they weren't coming for me.

Their bodies bobbed up and down. Their eyes rolled in their heads. They huddled together.

A few kids shook bony fists at me. A tall boy with skin peeling off his face kept spitting at the ground. Spitting and spitting, although nothing spilled from his mouth.

Why haven't they attacked?

Are they scared of me?

Still breathing hard, I climbed to my feet. I curled my hands into tight fists—ready for a fight—and kept my eyes on them.

What are they waiting for?

A small girl, her clothes hanging loosely on her, began to cough. She opened her mouth wide, coughing and choking. And I saw a large bug flutter out from inside her.

It buzzed loudly and floated in front of her face. The girl coughed some more, and another fat black bug shot out of her open mouth. The bugs made a droning hum and vanished into the night sky.

My fists were clenched so tight, my hands throbbed. I watched the zombie kids without blinking. There were at least a dozen of them against just one me.

I waited to see what they planned to do.

I uttered a gasp as the girl who had coughed up the insects shuffled toward me. She walked slowly, with stumbling steps, her mouth hanging open.

I stood frozen. I couldn't move.

The others remained in place and watched as she stepped up to me. Her dark eyes locked on mine. I stared into her cracked and peeling skin.

"Ohhh." I let out a low cry as she reached a bony finger up. She raised a finger and slowly trailed it down the side of my face.

A chill shook my body. Her finger traced my skin lightly.

I felt my legs about to collapse. My whole face tingled from the touch.

Her eyes burned into mine, as if trying to tell me something. A warning?

She lowered her finger and took a step back. She staggered toward her friends.

And then . . . to my shock . . . they all spun around at the same time. As if a signal had been given. Muttering and growling, they headed quickly toward the wall of cornstalks.

A few seconds later, they had disappeared into the corn.

I still didn't move. I stood there, fists clenched, my breaths wheezing loudly. I could still feel that hard, bony finger scratching down my cheek.

What was that about? Why did she do that? Why did they hurry away?

Finally, I forced my legs forward. I clicked on the light on my phone. And I pointed the light in front of me as I started to run.

My shoes sank into the dirt at the side of the cornfield as I picked up speed. I ran as if in a dream, following the bouncing, darting circle of light through the darkness.

Their ugly faces lingered in my mind as I raced back to the house. Their growls and low murmurs repeated in my ears. The girl coughing up bugs . . . touching my face with that bony finger . . .

Zombies.

Now I knew for certain they were there in the cornstalks. Not my imagination. Not raccoons or other animals. Not a trick of the moonlight over the corn.

Zombie kids.

It seemed as if I might run forever along the swaying stalks of the field, blacker than the night sky. I was gasping for breath when the porch lights of the house came into view.

The windows at the front of the house were dark. Had everyone gone to bed? Were they out looking for me?

I tore open the front door and stormed into the house. I wanted to shout to everyone to wake up, to come hear my story. But my voice caught in my dry, aching throat.

I grabbed the banister and pulled myself up the front staircase. My shoes thudded on the wooden steps.

I turned at the second-floor landing and raced down the dimly lit hall. The bedroom doors were closed. I grabbed the knob on Mila's door and pulled it open.

She was sitting on her bed with her laptop resting on her legs. She turned with a startled gasp as I charged into the room. "Todd?"

"I . . . I saw them!" I stammered, finally finding my voice. "I saw them, Mila. In the cornfield."

I ran up to her side and leaned over her. "I saw them all. You have to tell me the truth. Tell me the whole story. No more lying and trying to keep it secret. Do you hear me? You have to tell me everything!"

To my surprise, she burst into tears.

28

Mila sobbed and sobbed, letting the tears run down her cheeks. I waited for her to stop. But she kept sobbing with her head lowered as if I wasn't there.

I crossed the room and shook her gently by the shoulders. "Stop, Mila," I said softly. "Stop crying. You have to talk to me."

Her shoulders heaved up and down in my hands. She sobbed louder.

I had a sudden thought: *She's faking it.*

She's faking the tears because she doesn't want to talk to me. She has never wanted to tell me the truth.

I felt a flash of anger. But what could I do?

With her sobs ringing in my ears, I turned and strode out of her room.

I climbed to my attic room and kicked off my muddy shoes. Then I dropped onto the edge of my bed, took out my phone, and texted Shameka.

Are you awake? Can u talk?

A few seconds later, I read her reply:

Not really.

Huh? *Not really?* What did *that* mean?

I texted back:

I saw the zombies in the field tonight. Need u to explain.

Shameka texted back:

Don't start rumors.

I sighed. This wasn't getting me anywhere. I had to talk to her. I punched Shameka's number.

The phone rang once, then cut off.

I tried again. It went right to voice mail.

With another sigh, I tossed the phone onto my dresser and got dressed for bed.

Mila and Shameka knew something. Why wouldn't they talk to me?

The zombie kids knew something, too.

They knew I had seen them. Would they decide to come after me to shut me up?

At my desk in school the next morning, it was a struggle to keep my head up. It felt as heavy as a bowling ball. I wanted to curl up on the floor and go to sleep.

I hadn't slept all night. What was the point of even trying?

I couldn't stop thinking about the zombie kids and picturing their twisted, decaying faces and angry dark eyes.

Miss Opperman perched on the edge of her

desk. She was reading something from her iPad to the class. But I didn't hear a word of it.

Too many thoughts were bouncing around in my brain. Her words sounded like a jangle of noise in the background.

I turned and saw that, next to me, Owen was staring at me.

Did I look weird? Could he tell that I was messed up?

Everyone laughed at something Miss Opperman read. I pretended to laugh, too.

I need to know the truth, I decided.

And suddenly, I knew exactly what I had to do.

A girl came to the classroom door to say that
Mrs. Bane, the principal, wanted to see Miss
Opperman. Our teacher started to the door.
"Read over your science notes while I'm away,"
she said.

The door closed behind her.

I leaned over toward Owen. "I'm going to
sneak out," I whispered.

His eyes went wide.

"I have to find out something."

He frowned at me. "Like what?" he whispered back.

"Like what's in Room 5-Z," I said.

Owen swallowed. He leaned his head closer
and whispered in my ear, "Don't look for trouble."

"I'm not," I replied. "But—"

He glanced to the door. Miss Opperman was
turning a corner down the hall.

"It's better to mind your own business," he
said. "Seriously."

"I can't," I said. I raised a finger to my lips, meaning for him not to say anything.

Most kids had their heads down, reading over their science notes. A few were chatting quietly.

I climbed up from my seat and strode quickly to the door. I kept my eyes straight ahead, hoping no one would say anything to me.

I slipped out into the hall and gazed both ways. No one here. I didn't want to run into Miss Opperman, coming from the principal's office.

I pressed myself against the wall and moved as silently as I could toward the front of the school.

Holding my breath, I turned the corner into the main hall. I gasped as a classroom door swung open.

Caught?

No. The door closed as quickly as it had opened. No one stepped out.

I sucked in another deep breath and practically tiptoed the rest of the way. Tiptoed past my locker. Tiptoed right up to Room 5-Z. I read the stenciled room number on the classroom door.

Well, here I am.

My mouth was suddenly as dry as cotton, and my legs felt rubbery and weak. I stared hard at the words ROOM 5-Z, gathering my courage.

Finally, I reached for the door handle. Began to turn it.

And stopped.

Oh, wow! What is THAT?

I ducked behind my locker door as two men in blue uniforms pushed open the front entrance. They were hauling a large metal cart between them.

The cart banged into the hall, its wheels squeaking on the tile floor. It passed right by me. The men had their eyes straight ahead. One of them was talking on a phone as he pushed the cart.

The cart was piled high with metal tins. Like the big cans that a ham comes in. The cans rattled and bounced as the men rolled the cart along the hall.

As they rumbled past, I read the labels on the cans: CANNED MEAT.

"Huh?" Why did that name seem familiar?

Where were they taking it?

I poked my head out from behind the locker door to get a better look.

They didn't go far. They stopped in front of Room 5-Z.

The man at the front of the cart knocked on

the door. He didn't wait for an answer. He pushed open the door.

The voices inside the room stopped. Then I heard soft applause. A few cheers.

The men rolled the cart into the classroom and shut the door behind them. I could hear voices again inside the room and people moving around.

I stepped away from my locker and stared at Room 5-Z. All those tins of canned meat . . . delivered right to that room.

Now I knew what was in that room. I knew the zombie kids were in there. The kids that had arrived on that disgusting bus my first morning.

The zombie kids are in Room 5-Z, and they bring them canned meat. That's what they eat instead of human flesh!

Yes, I had it all figured out. But was I right?

I had to make sure.

By now, Miss Opperman probably knew I had left the classroom. Maybe she was out looking for me. Maybe she had reported me to Mrs. Bane, and they were both looking for me. But I didn't care.

I had to see for myself what was on the other side of that door.

I pressed my back against the wall and waited for the men to leave. I tensed when I heard footsteps far down the hall. But they grew fainter and then disappeared.

I stared at the door to Room 5-Z. *Hurry up, guys.*

A few minutes later, the door swung open. The

two men pushed the empty cart out of the room and rolled it to the school entrance.

I watched them push it outside. Then I made my move.

I forced myself away from the wall and took a few quick steps toward Room 5-Z. I stopped at the door. I could hear voices inside.

My hand trembled as I grabbed the doorknob. My whole body gave a hard shudder. I pulled my hand back.

Am I really doing this?

I knew I didn't have a choice.

I wrapped my hand around the knob again— and shoved the door open.

My stomach lurched. Just as I had guessed. The zombie kids were in there, hunched around low wooden tables.

Zombie kids . . . Zombie kids . . . Real zombie kids.

And sitting across from each other at a table near the back . . . I saw Mila and Shameka.

31

"Oh noooo!"

A scream burst from my throat.

The zombie kids all swung around to the door. Mila's eyes went wide. She scrambled to her feet. Her chair went crashing to the floor.

Shameka jumped up, too. Her mouth dropped open. Staring at me, she began to shake her head, as if warning me I shouldn't be there.

I *knew* I shouldn't be there. But here I was. And there was no way I could unsee what I was seeing.

My legs trembled. I realized I was still squeezing the doorknob.

I had guessed right. The zombie kids were all in Room 5-Z.

But what were Shameka and Mila doing in here?

The teacher was not a zombie. He was a tall, bald-headed guy, big as a football left tackle. He wore a baggy gray sweatshirt and black sweatpants.

He was at the back of the room. When he saw

me, he screamed, "Get out!" Then he came charging at me, head lowered like a bull.

I uttered another cry and whirled away.

My shoes hammered the floor as I ran. I shoved my arms in front of me—and banged open the front entrance door. And kept going.

Down the stairs and across the grass in front of the school. I ran full speed toward the road.

I didn't slow when I heard shouts behind me. But I glanced back and saw Mila and Shameka chasing me.

"Todd—wait!"

"Todd—stop! We can explain!"

Explain what?

Explain why you're in the zombie classroom?

"Todd—listen to us!"

"Wait up!"

Tall grass ran along the side of the road. I tried to leap over it. Missed. Lost my balance.

While I struggled to stay on my feet, Mila dove at me. She wrapped her hands around my legs from behind and tackled me to the ground.

I landed hard on my side and felt a stab of pain as the air whooshed out of me. I lay there in the grass, struggling to get my breath.

Mila held on to my legs and Shameka bent over me, grabbed my shoulders, and held me in place.

"L-let go!" I gasped when I could finally breathe again. "Let go of me!"

"You have to listen to us, Todd," Mila said. "You have to let us explain."

"Explain what?" I cried. I shoved Shameka's hands away. "Explain why you've never told me the truth? Why you lied to me since I arrived? Explain why you wanted me to think I was going crazy?"

"Todd, please—" Mila started.

"Why were you two in that classroom?" I screamed. "Why were you both in the zombie classroom?"

Shameka laughed, a bitter, cold laugh. "Can't you guess?"

32

A blue SUV rumbled past us on the road. I wanted to signal to it, to wave and cry out for help. I suddenly realized I was *afraid* of the two girls.

"Will you just stop screaming and let us explain?" Mila said.

"Do I have a choice?" I muttered.

A scrawny gray squirrel started across the road. It stopped in the middle and watched us for a moment. Then it ran into the tall grass on the other side.

Mila swept back her hair. "Listen," she said. "We *did* tell you the truth. We told you the truth the other day at Shameka's farm."

"The school bus story is true," Shameka said. "The kids from Michigan stopped at Mila's cornfield, and something happened to them. Somehow, they died in the cornfield. They died, but they didn't go away. They became the living dead."

"How?" I demanded. "How did they die?"

"We don't know," Mila said. "We don't have a clue, Todd. We only know it happened. When they finally came out of the cornfield, they were zombies."

"The kids in Room 5-Z are the zombies from the cornfield," Shameka continued the story. "The school has to take them. The law here says all kids have to go to school. They come to school on their bus, and the school feeds them."

"Canned meat," I said.

They both nodded. "Canned meat. So they don't have to eat human flesh," Shameka said.

They both studied me. I knew they were watching to see if I believed them.

I believed them.

"So why did you two lie to me?" I demanded. "Mila, why did your whole family lie to me?"

"You just arrived here," she said. "We didn't want you to be afraid of staying with us. Also . . ."

"The town doesn't want word to get out," Shameka finished Mila's sentence. "If people find out about the zombie kids, Moose Hollow will be ruined."

"People will flood the town," Mila said, "coming to see the zombies. Reporters will come . . . TV people . . . Our town would never be the same. So we try to keep it quiet."

They went silent again, watching me.

"Okay," I said. "I believe you. But you still haven't explained one thing . . . one *big* thing."

"What big thing?" Mila asked.

I took a breath. "Why were you two in the class with the zombies? You weren't on that school bus from Michigan. Why were you in that room with all the zombies?"

33

Mila kicked a clump of dirt. She didn't raise her eyes.

Shameka crossed her arms in front of her. She made a sour face and didn't answer my question.

"Well? Go ahead," I said. "You told me part of it. You have to tell me the rest!"

"Okay, okay," Mila muttered. "We're . . . we're zombies, too."

"Huh?" I gasped. "That's crazy. You don't look like zombies. You don't live in the cornfield."

"Believe us," Shameka said softly. "They made us zombies, too."

"If you leave them alone, they won't bother you," Mila said. "But—"

"That's what Owen told me in school," I said.

"Owen was right," Mila said. "But Shameka and I . . . we went after the zombies in the cornfield. We followed them and spied on them. And they caught us snooping. They . . ." Her voice trailed off.

"They dragged us into the cornfield," Shameka said, shaking her head. "We couldn't escape them."

"We died, too," Mila said, her voice trembling. "We don't even remember how. All we remember is, we weren't alive anymore. When we walked back out of the cornfield, we were the living dead."

A chill shook my whole body.

The trees began to shake overhead, as if reacting to what the girls had told me. The rustle of leaves didn't drown out my horrified thoughts.

"So you two . . ." I couldn't finish my sentence. They both nodded.

"But . . . but . . ." I sputtered. "You don't look like zombies. And you both live at home with your parents."

"Yes, they let us live at home," Shameka replied. "As long as we keep their secret. They know we're not part of their group—"

"We can't explain why we haven't changed," Mila said. "Why do we still look like ourselves? It's all a horrible mystery. But it really doesn't matter. Because we are not . . ." Her voice caught in her throat. "We are not alive, like you."

A small white van roared past us on the road. The driver gave us two short honks of the horn.

I could see the sadness on both girls' faces. I struggled to think of something to say. But I was stumped.

And then their expressions changed. Their eyes

119

went cold. Their mouths tightened into straight lines.

"You snooped, too, Todd," Shameka said. "You spied on the kids. You trespassed on their bus."

"You should have stayed away," Mila said. "We tried to keep you away from the truth. But . . . you didn't listen. You saw too much."

Mila grabbed my arm. "Come with us, Todd," she said.

"Huh? Come where?"

She tightened her grip. "Into the woods. Come on. It won't hurt for long."

34

"Whoa! Wait a minute!" I tried to swipe my arm away. But she held on with surprising strength.

I tried to run, but Shameka blocked my path.

"We told you everything," she said in a low voice from deep in her throat. "Everything. Now you have to come with us."

"You saw too much, Todd," Mila said. "Don't blame us. We have no choice."

"No. Wait. Please—" I pleaded.

Mila's hand tightened even more. My whole arm began to throb. I ducked and twisted. But I couldn't free myself from her steel grip.

"Todd, don't try to resist. Join us," she whispered. I could barely hear her over the rush of the wind. "Just think how awesome it will be. You will be with us *forever*."

"N-no!" I stammered.

"Of course you want to do it," Shameka said. Her voice lowered to a growl. "You do, Todd. You do."

"No! Let go of me!" I screamed.

But Mila dragged me forward, onto the road. I tightened my leg muscles and dug in my heels. Tried to hold back. But she was dragging me, dragging me to the trees on the other side.

"Don't be afraid. It doesn't hurt for long," Mila said. "And then you will be immortal, too." She gave a hard tug that nearly pulled me off my feet.

We had crossed the road. The shadows of the tall trees rolled over me. As if night was falling.

"You will be like us, Todd," Mila said, her hand digging into my skin as she forced me into the woods. "We will live forever."

"Nooooo!" I screamed. "Noooo. Let gooooo!"

"Forever," Mila repeated. "Don't be afraid."

35

Shameka grabbed my other arm. The two of them pulled me off the road into the deep shadow of the trees. "Please . . ." I whispered. "Please . . ."

All three of us stopped when we heard a shout.

I took advantage of the girls' surprise to jerk my arms free. I spun around—and saw the bike rolling toward us. Squinting hard, I recognized Skipper on his electric bike, coming on fast.

"Skipper—go away!" Mila cried. "I mean it! Go away!"

She made a grab for me and missed.

I lurched back onto the road.

Skipper stopped in front of me. "Quick! Jump on!" he shouted, slapping the seat right behind him.

I didn't need a second invitation. I leaped onto the bike.

He shot the bike forward before I was seated. I grabbed his sides from behind and held on tight as we zoomed away.

"Skipper to the rescue!" he shouted over the rush of wind in our faces.

I twisted around and saw Mila and Shameka standing in the middle of the road, hands on their waists, watching as I escaped.

We whirred away, bumping over the rutted country road. In a few seconds, the two girls were far in the distance.

Standing on the pedals, Skipper leaned over the handlebars, and we picked up speed. Bouncing on the seat, I gripped the sides of his denim jacket and struggled to hold on.

How did I feel? Relieved, of course. And happy to get away from my zombie cousin and her zombie friend. But my brain swirled with questions. Where were we going? Where was Skipper taking me?

I didn't have to wait long to find out.

The road twisted through shadowy woods. And then the thick clumps of trees gave way to empty brown fields.

Skipper swerved the bike sharply as a long gray SUV roared toward us. As it passed, I saw three or four kids in the backseats, all staring out at us.

Clouds moved away from the sun, and the fields brightened to gold. I squinted against the sharp blue of the sky.

When my eyes adjusted to the new light, I saw

a cornfield up ahead. Skipper slowed the bike as we came near it. Then he turned and guided the bike along the side of the tall brown stalks.

"Hey—!" I tapped Skipper's sides with both hands. "Hey—is this *your* cornfield? Are we back at your farm?"

He didn't answer. I'm not sure he could hear me.

At the back end of the field, he made a sharp right turn.

I gasped as I saw the bus up ahead. The battered gray bus parked once again at the back of the field, tilting to one side.

"No!" I shouted. "What are we *doing* here? I don't want to be here. Skipper—turn around!"

He turned his head to face me. I gasped when I saw the cold expression in his eyes. "Todd, did you think I was alive? Did I fool a city kid like you? Did you really think Mila and Shameka were the only ones chasing zombies in the cornfield? I spied on them, too. And they caught me snooping . . ."

My breath caught in my throat. I couldn't answer.

The bike stopped short with a screech. The tires sank into the soft dirt at the edge of the field.

I brushed my hair down with both hands. Rubbed my eyes. And saw the kids step out from the cornstalks.

The zombie kids. Gray-skinned, blank eyes

rolling in their heads, mouths hanging open hungrily . . . The zombie kids dragging themselves from the field.

How did they get here so quickly? Here they were, waiting for me.

Skipper twisted around again and gave me the same cold, blank stare. "Last stop," he said.

36

Skipper gave me a soft push, and I slid off the bike and landed on my feet.

"Wait—!" I cried. But he leaned forward and kicked the pedals. His bike tires sent up a cloud of dirt as he sped away.

The zombie kids didn't hang back this time. They moved quickly to surround me.

They grunted excitedly, their jaws swung up and down, and their eyes rolled in their heads.

"Please—" I choked out.

But two tall zombie boys bumped up against me. One slid his hand around my waist. The other grabbed my shoulder.

"Let go! Please—let go!" My voice came out high and shrill.

I tried to pull free. But they were too strong.

Their soft grunts rose up all around me. *"Hunh hunh hunh . . ."* A chant from deep in their throats. *"Hunh hunh hunh . . ."*

The stalks brushed against me, poking me, scratching me, as they pulled me deeper into the field. The two zombie boys shoved me forward. I saw a bare spot up ahead. A small circle. A break in the rows of dry brown stalks.

They pushed me into the opening. And two others stepped out to greet me. Mila and Shameka.

I opened my mouth to plead with them, to beg them to let me go. But the words choked in my throat. I couldn't make a sound.

Their faces were cold, their jaws set hard, eyes frozen on me as they stepped up to me. "It only hurts for a little while," Shameka whispered.

The zombie kids grunted as if answering her.

"A few seconds," Mila said, "and then you will be with us forever, Todd."

I twisted my whole body and tried to squirm free. But the two tall zombie boys didn't loosen their grip.

"Please . . . Please . . ." I finally found my voice. "I won't tell anyone about you," I said. "I promise. I'll never mention this to anyone."

"*Hunh hunh hunh . . .*" came the growling chant, rising over the tall corn.

"A few seconds," Mila repeated. Her eyes were as cold and dead as the other zombies. "A few seconds, Todd."

Doomed.

The word flashed into my mind, for the first time ever.

I'm doomed.

And then, my heart seemed to skip a beat.

I had a desperate, last-second idea.

37

"Hunnnh hunh hunnnh . . ."

The zombie kids moved their circle tighter. The sour smell rose up from their bodies and washed over me. I struggled to not choke on the odor.

I lowered a hand to my jeans pocket. I could feel the harmonica in there. Wrong pocket. The other pocket held my plastic lighter. The lighter my grandfather had given me for good luck.

Good luck.

That's just what I needed now.

I had never used the lighter. I'd never even made it flame.

But I had a desperate idea to use it now.

What if I set the dry cornstalks on fire?

Would the flames frighten the zombie kids away? Would a fire give me a chance to run? If the stalks flare up and the flames surround them, will the zombie kids run?

I slid my hand into my jeans pocket and wrapped my fingers around the old lighter.

Did it still work?

I gazed at my cousin Mila and her friend. Shameka. They stared hard at me, not blinking, not moving, as the zombies closed in.

Gripping the lighter tightly, I pulled it out of my pocket. Before anyone could grab it, I shot my arm out and raised the lighter to the nearest cornstalk.

And I clicked it hard.

38

Nothing happened.

It didn't flame.

I clicked it again.

Again.

I shook the lighter hard, then clicked it. CLICK. CLICK. CLICK.

No flame. Nothing. The lighter didn't work.

With a hard swipe, a zombie boy slapped it out of my hand. I watched it hit the ground and bounce between the stalks.

Can I run? I asked myself.

Their circle tightened around me. No way I could break through.

Mila and Shameka gripped my arms and held me in place. "It will only hurt for a little while," Mila said again. "Then you will live with us in the corn forever."

"Think about that," Shameka said. "Don't you want to live forever?"

I *was* thinking about it.

"Hunnh hunh hunh . . ."

The low growls and grunts grew louder, ringing in my ears until my whole head throbbed. I shut my eyes, trying to force away the pain.

Then I opened them and turned to Mila and Shameka. "Hey, wait a minute," I said. "Hold on."

Their cold eyes met mine.

"I want to ask you one question," I said. I slid the harmonica from my jeans pocket and held it up.

"What's your question?" Mila demanded.

"Well . . . if I let you turn me into a zombie," I said, "can I play my harmonica in your band?"

They looked at each other.

Shameka nodded.

"Yes, sure. Fine," Mila said.

"Okay, then," I said. "Let's do it!"

EPILOGUE FROM SLAPPY

Well . . . I knew Todd was *dying* to be in a band. I guess he got his wish. Hahaha!

Don't ever say my stories don't have a happy ending!

I hope you enjoyed Todd's story. I hope you didn't think it was too *corny*! Haha.

I'll be back soon with another Goosebumps story.

Remember, this is *SlappyWorld*.

You only *scream* in it!

SLAPPYWORLD #15:
JUDY AND THE BEAST

Read on for a preview!

1

I jumped and cried out as the monster roared in my face. I shot both hands up and tried to push it away.

"Get back, Ira!" I shouted. "You're not funny."

My brother laughed and lowered his wooden monster to his side. He took a step back. Then he waved the monster at me again. "It's pretty awesome, don't you think, Judy?"

"You're *sick*," I said. "You think it's normal to spend all your time in the garage building monsters?"

He nodded. "Yeah. Normal."

I shoved the tall wooden thing out of my way and crossed to the open garage door. "Sick," I repeated.

I turned to the shelves against the wall. "Look at them all. A dozen monsters. And what do you do with them, Ira? You don't put on puppet shows or anything, or show them off to people. Your monsters just sit there on the shelves, staring at the driveway."

Ira laughed again. He has an annoying laugh. Like gravel scraping in his throat. "They're waiting to attack," he said. "When I give the signal, my monsters will take over the town."

He picked up a small square of sandpaper and began smoothing it over his monster's wooden back. Our garage has every kind of tool and supply. A lathe. Two different kinds of saws. A whole wall of hammers and pliers and chisels and things I don't even know what they are.

That's because our dad is a carpenter.

He does useful work. He doesn't use his tools to build monster after monster.

"Ira, you're fifteen," I said. "Why don't you play video games like everyone else in your class? Or, if you want to build stuff, why don't you build model airplanes or cars?"

"I like monsters," he replied. He raised the monster and started to gently sand one of its long ears.

I shrugged. "Yeah. Okay. I get it, Ira. Sulphur Falls is a boring place to live. You need a hobby."

"It's not just a hobby," he said. He carried the monster to the shelves and sat it down next to one of the others. "These are going to be valuable some day."

He straightened a fat, piglike creation and wiped dust off its broad head. "I'm going to start a monster YouTube channel and sell them."

Clouds rolled over the sun, and the light dimmed in the garage. It was spring, but the breezes coming down from the mountain felt as chilly as winter.

I straightened my sweater and hugged myself in the sudden cold. "You know what?" I said. "Your monsters would look better if you painted their faces. Why don't you let me do it? You know I love to paint. I could make them a lot creepier."

He shook his head. "No way, Judy. Forget about that. I think they're scarier *without* faces. You have to use your imagination."

I opened my mouth to argue with him. But I heard someone calling my name. I turned and saw Dad striding from the house.

Dad is short and round and white haired, even though he isn't that old. His friends in town call him Walrus because his white mustache droops down the sides of his mouth like walrus tusks.

Dad's stomach bounced under his overalls as he walked. He wears denim overalls with lots of pockets for his tools and red-and-black flannel shirts. And the front of him is usually covered in sawdust, so it looks like he has terrible dandruff.

"Hey, Dad," I said. "What's up?"

He stopped at the garage door. The wind ruffled his white hair. "Hi, Judy," he said. "I'm afraid I have bad news."

Before we get to Dad's bad news, I should start out by telling you about me and my family and all that beginning-story stuff. I'm afraid I was so busy arguing with Ira about his monsters, I got a little ahead of myself.

You probably figured out my name is Judy. Judy Glassman. I'm twelve and my brother Ira the Monster Maker is fifteen.

After our parents split up, Mom decided to move to England. We visit her as often as we can. Dad moved Ira and me here to Sulphur Falls, Wyoming.

It's a tiny ski town at the bottom of Black Rock Mountain. The mountain is snow-covered most of the year, and the skiing is good. Otherwise, why would people come here?

Dad moved us to get back to his roots. He grew up on a ranch in Wyoming. He wanted us to have a fresh start. And he argued, "People in small towns need carpenters, too."

Ira and I wanted to stay back East. We didn't want to leave our friends. But how could we argue with Dad? Besides, Ira and I are not exactly timid. I'm not bragging, but I'd say we're always up for a new adventure.

And living in this tiny town at the foot of Black Rock Mountain is definitely an adventure. With the sun behind it, the shadow of the mountain falls over the entire town.

It's dark most of the day, and the mountain air is at least ten degrees colder than anywhere else. I'm so happy that spring has come around because it means a few warm days before the cold returns.

I followed Dad into the house. We have a wood-burning stove in the middle of the kitchen, and it keeps the room warm and toasty. We sat down across from each other at the breakfast counter.

I tapped my fingers on the white countertop. "Okay, let me have it," I said. "What's your bad news?"

Dad tugged at the sides of his walrus mustache. "Well, you know what happens every spring, Judy," he began. "Time for me to go up to Baker Grendel's house."

I groaned. "Again? Do you really have to go this year?"

He nodded. "You know I do. The snow is melting, and the roads up the mountain are passable. Grendel is expecting me."

Baker Grendel and his wife, Hilda, have a huge mansion at the top of the mountain. At least, that's what I've heard. I've never seen it.

Dad travels up there every spring to do repairs and carpentry work for them. He usually stays up there for a week. One year, he got snowed in and was stuck up there for nearly two weeks.

He ran a hand through his thick white hair. "Baker and his wife, Hilda, are strange," he said. "But they pay very well."

I groaned and rolled my eyes. "And I suppose you're taking Ira with you as always?" I said. "You're taking Ira and leaving me behind with Mrs. Hardwell?"

Dad's cheeks turned pink. He knows Mrs. Hardwell and I don't get along. To put it mildly.

Mrs. Hardwell is our housekeeper, and she's always on my case. She's boring and strict and too serious. And she never wants me to have any fun.

Dad avoided my stare. He glanced out the kitchen window to the backyard. "Yes," he said finally. "I'm taking Ira."

I slammed my fist on the table. "No fair!" I shouted. "No fair, Dad."

"Judy, please—"

"You take Ira every year," I said. "It's my turn. I want to go, too. How can you be so unfair?"

"Ira helps me with the work," Dad said. "He

knows the tools from working on his wooden monsters."

"I know tools—" I started.

He raised a hand, motioning for me to stop. "I can't take you both," he said. "The ride up to the mountaintop is just too treacherous. You know I can't even take the jeep. The melting snow makes the dirt road too slippery. I have to take a horse and wagon. You'd hate it, Judy."

"Try me," I said. "I won't hate it. I promise, Dad." I could feel my anger tightening my throat. Dad's reasons didn't make sense.

Why couldn't I go? Why did it always have to be Ira?

"I don't want to stay with Mrs. Hardwell," I shouted. "She's horrid!"

A voice behind me made me gasp. "You can't mean that, Judy." Mrs. Hardwell appeared at the kitchen door.

She walked in shaking her head. Her short, straight black hair bobbed with her head, and her tiny black bird eyes were locked on me. A smile spread across her pale narrow face, but I knew it was totally fake.

"Sorry you feel that way," she said. She speaks with a smooth, velvety voice. Also fake. "It's because you think you can run wild when your father isn't here. I have to keep you in line."

About the Author

R.L. Stine says he gets to scare people all over the world. So far, his books have sold more than 400 million copies, making him one of the most popular children's authors in history. The Goosebumps series has more than 150 titles and has inspired a TV series and two motion pictures. R.L. himself is a character in the movies! He has also written the teen series Fear Street, and the Mostly Ghostly and Nightmare Room series. He is currently writing a series of graphic novels entitled Just Beyond. R.L. Stine lives in New York City with his wife, Jane, an editor and publisher. You can learn more about him at rlstine.com.

Catch the MOST WANTED Goosebumps® villains UNDEAD OR ALIVE!

scholastic.com/goosebumps

GBMW42

THE SCARIEST PLACE ON EARTH!

The Original Bone-Chilling Series

—with Exclusive Author Interviews!

THE ORIGINAL Goosebumps BOOKS
WITH AN ALL-NEW LOOK!

GET YOUR HANDS ON THEM BEFORE THEY GET THEIR HANDS ON YOU!

CONTINUE THE FRIGHT AT THE GOOSEBUMPS SITE
scholastic.com/goosebumps

FANS OF GOOSEBUMPS CAN:

- PLAY THE GHOULISH GAME:
  GOOSEBUMPS: SLAPPY'S DROP DEAD HOUSE

- LEARN ABOUT NEW BOOKS AND TERRIFYING CLASSICS

- TAKE A QUIZ AND LEARN WHICH TYPE OF MONSTER YOU ARE!

- LEARN ABOUT THE AUTHOR WHO STARTED IT ALL: R.L. STINE

SCHOLASTIC